ANIMAL ACCOMPLICE

PET WHISPERER P.I.
BOOK 18

MOLLY FITZ

AUTHOR'S NOTE

This is it! Angie and Octo-Cat's final adventure. Thank you for giving them space in your brain—and your heart—for eighteen books and two shorts!

Just to make sure you haven't missed anything, I've listed the full series order below and placed stars next to the shorts to make sure you've got them.

Kitty Confidential

<u>Terrier Transgressions</u>

<u>Hairless Harassment</u>

<u>Dog-Eared Delinquent</u>

<u>The Cat Caper</u>

<u>Chihuahua Conspiracy</u>

<u>Raccoon Racketeer</u>

<u>Himalayan Hazard</u>

*<u>Meowy Christmas Mayhem</u>

<u>Hoppy Holiday Homicide</u>

<u>Retriever Ransom</u>

<u>Lawless Litter</u>

<u>Legal Seagull</u>

*<u>Black Cat Benefit</u>

<u>Grizzly Grievance</u>

<u>Persian Penalty</u>

<u>Deer Duplicity</u>

<u>Scheming Sphynx</u>

<u>Honeymoon Hearsay</u>

<u>Animal Accomplice</u>

I hope you'll enjoy Animal Accomplice and be happy with where everyone ends up by the close of this series.

Also, let me assure you that the official Pet Whisperer P.I. series may be coming to an end, but two unique spinoffs are in the works! I also plan to release an epilogue story this year to show how everyone is doing in their new lives.

ABOUT THIS BOOK

The jig is up. Someone knows my secret.

What starts as mild online harassment soon turns much more dire when my blackmailer reveals irrefutable proof of my ability to talk to animals, promising to expose me whether I like it or not.

I've always lived life on my own terms, but if word were to get out about my secret superpower, I know better than anyone that things would never be the same... for me or anyone I love.

With the stakes higher than ever, Octo-Cat and I decide to take on one last case. First we must reveal the identity of my anonymous bully, and then we'll have to ask ourselves the hardest question yet: Where do we go from here?

1

My name is Angie Longfellow, and I lead a pretty great life. For the longest time, I had trouble finding my path, racking up associate degrees and building my resume like nobody's business.

I never would have suspected my crummy job as a paralegal for the local law firm would have led to my happily ever after, but it brought me both my husband and my very special, *very secret* ability.

So, yeah, I can talk to animals, a fact that more or less rules my day-to-day life.

It all started when a faulty coffee maker zapped me unconscious at a will reading, only for me to be awoken by the deceased's cat—who also just so happened to be her primary beneficiary. With vile tuna breath, he informed me that his old lady had not died of natural causes and that it was up to me to help him solve the murder and bring her killer to justice.

At first I could only talk to him—to Octo-Cat—but now I can talk to pretty much any animal or insect that is willing to talk back. My regular entourage includes that original talking tabby, my husband's two hairless cats Jacques and Jillianne, our newly adopted kitten Charlene, and Pringle the raccoon who lives in a swanky set of tree houses in the backyard.

Paisley the rescue Chihuahua moved out when Nan went to live with her new husband Grant. I miss having her in the house, but I still see her nearly every day, along with Grant's rescue bunny—a Holland Lop named E.B.

It's strange not living with my grandmother anymore, but I do love married life. Charles works long hours as the senior partner at the law firm, and I don't have much to do, given that my P.I. business rarely has any clients.

So in the meantime, Nan is teaching me to be domestic. I'm pretty good at cleaning the house, but my cooking leaves much to be desired. Still, I have a lot of time to figure things out since Charles works such long hours.

To fill my time, I also read several books per week, which is kind of a dream come true. Except it's starting to wear on me.

I love reading about others' adventures—don't get me wrong—but I also want to live my own. I was the main character here, not some simple spectator. Lately, though, my life doesn't have a whole lot of plot.

Strange how having all your dreams come true can turn out to be so boring. It's like I have nothing left to strive for, that I already have everything I've ever wanted—and then some.

Between Charles's cushy paycheck and Octo-Cat's trust fund, we're more than covered financially, but still, I'd like to make my business a success for my own satisfaction.

There's just two problems with that. First, Nan and my mom took it upon themselves to register my firm with the state government as Pet Whisperer P.I., which means I'm stuck with the name. Second, I'm not the sole owner. Octo-Cat is my partner, and he's not always the easiest to work with.

In fact, he doesn't want to do any work at all,

not since he piggybacked on my wedding to marry his long-time, long-distance girlfriend, Grizabella, the former show cat. Then right after that, we subsequently adopted Charlene, the little lost kitten Charles and I found on our honeymoon.

Now our Octavius is a full-time doting dad and a constant critic of yours truly. I have a feeling *that* will never change, no matter how much I might want it to.

* * *

"You're slouching," Octo-Cat growled shortly after entering our shared office.

I straightened my spine then let out a long, frustrated sigh and clicked my laptop shut. Twisting in my desk chair, I turned to face my feline partner. "Where's Charlene?" I asked with one eyebrow quirked in question.

Octo-Cat sat and idly licked at a paw. "The nudists have her for late-morning classes."

"I really wish you'd stop calling the Sphynx cats that." I groaned. Still, I found it adorable that the three cats had rallied around our new arrival, even going so far as to homeschool her. I had no idea what they taught her during these catting lessons, but everyone seemed more or less content, so I didn't pry.

He dropped his paw to the ground and stared at me with wide amber eyes. "Do you prefer I go back to referring to them as the interlopers?"

"But you're all getting along now," I argued, drumming my fingers on my knee as I thought about how I might turn this conversation around before my kitty partner became too agitated.

He just shook his head. "Thus the new nickname. You can't deny the fact they're naked, Angela. If they wanted to grow fur, they would have done it by now."

I chose not to acknowledge that with anything more than an exacerbated eye roll.

Octo-Cat shifted his eyes toward the desk then back to me in the chair. Thankfully, it was he who changed the subject, although it was definitely one I didn't care for. "Are you really done with work already? It's hardly past breakfast time."

"I'm just not making any progress, and I feel bad spending Charles's money when the ads clearly aren't working."

"You never felt bad about spending my money," he pointed out with a holier-than-thou expression.

Heat rushed to my cheeks. "That was different,"

I admitted, glancing down at my lap before returning my gaze to him in embarrassment.

"Oh?" Octo-Cat tilted his head to the side as he studied me. "Then go ahead. Please do tell me how."

"Well, you're my business partner, and it's not exactly like you work for your income," I mumbled meekly; my confidence could never match his and that often became a problem.

The tabby scoffed at this. "I don't work? Ha. Is that so? I'll have you know that I work very hard keeping tabs on you all day."

I pressed both palms to my thighs and then stood. "Look, I'm not trying to start a fight or anything. I'm just feeling discouraged is all."

"I already told you. You've been doing the work for free for far too long. Nobody wants to pay for it now."

I sighed. Octo-Cat was a pretty good sleuth, but he was a terrible businessman. I wasn't much better, but I still knew I could learn. My cat seemed to think he was infallible in this and all things.

I stopped at the door and turned back to him. "It's not that—"

"Not to mention, the one time you did have a paying client, you pinned the crime on him!" he shouted as if it were the silliest thing he'd ever heard.

"He was guilty," I argued right back. Frankly, I was done with this conversation, but I knew Octo-Cat wouldn't drop it until he was satisfied, meaning I was stuck for the moment. "Was I supposed to turn a blind eye just because he was paying us?"

My cat shrugged. "It was a bad business decision. That's all I'm saying."

Was my cat right? Was I hopeless at this whole business thing? Well, it wasn't like I could go out and find another private investigation firm to hire me on salary. This kind of work was pretty much freelance, which meant if I wanted to continue as a detective, I'd have to get a whole lot better at the business side. *Ugh.* Perhaps it was time to simply admit defeat. All my other dreams had come true, so why did I continue to cling to the only one that hadn't?

"Maybe I should ask Charles for some paralegal work," I admitted with a sigh. "I was good at that. Plus, having something to do with myself would make it so I don't feel quite so useless."

My cat growled at me. "You are not leaving me here alone all day. What if I need fresh water? What if someone comes to the door? What then, Angela?"

I ignored him and headed down the hall in the direction of the grand staircase. Perhaps I'd feel better about this whole failed businesswoman thing once I'd had a bit of lunch.

Was ten a.m. too early for my second meal of the day?

2

After heating up some frozen waffles and slathering them with both butter and blueberry syrup, I felt a little better. But once I'd managed to finish eating them, I found myself with a slight stomach ache.

Note to self: *ten is, in fact, too early for lunch. Also you are not a hobbit, so no more second breakfasts.*

Octo-Cat now lay snoozing in a sunbeam while Jacques and Jillianne looked after Charlene, which gave me a bit of time to myself. I'd just finished my current read last night, so instead of starting something new, I decided to do a little extra work at my desk. After all, I'd only stopped earlier because of Octo-Cat's intrusion.

With a quick prayer to the heavens, I lifted the lid of my laptop and did the same thing I always did when starting a work session—checked my messages for any new client inquiries.

And just like always... digital crickets.

I sighed and moved on to scroll my newsfeed. I'd started a new profile for the business and made sure to follow other private investigators only. Seeing what was working for them was meant to inspire and motivate me. Instead, it only made me feel more hopeless with regards to my own floundering firm.

I was just reading an article detailing how a P.I. duo in the Midwest added murder mystery dinner parties to their repertoire, when a little red notification popped up on my screen.

Excitement surged through my veins.

Was this it? The new client who would turn my entire practice around?

I clicked eagerly and waited while the social media site pulled up one of my geo-targeted ads. Someone had left a comment.

I'd clearly listed my info and availability in a pinned post at the top of my page, but maybe this person was so desperate for help, they skipped researching me and went straight to reaching out.

Yeah, I liked that. My services weren't only needed, they were now in demand.

Dancing in my seat, I dragged my eyes down the page to read the comment from my brand-spanking-new client and possibly my new biggest fan.

The username was Charm—no last name—just Charm, and the comment said: *I know who you are. I know your secret, and soon everyone else will too.*

Dread roiled in my gut. Who was this Charm, and why had they decided to mess with me? Surely, this whole thing was just some stupid coincidence. Granted, I hadn't always been as careful as I should when it came to protecting my secret ability, but...

No, no way.

I clicked on Charm's name to open their profile, but the privacy settings had been cranked all the way to the max, and the profile snapshot of an ocean told me absolutely nothing.

With shaking hands, I navigated back to my ad. I should have simply deleted the comment, blocked the user, and moved on with my day.

But I couldn't.

I had to know more.

Who are you? I typed, waited for a beat, then added, *And what are you talking about?*

The response was almost immediate: *You don't know me, but you do know what I'm talking about.*

I bit my lip and slunk back in my chair. What were the chances that Charm was making everything up? And how could they possibly know my secret if they didn't even know me?

And most importantly of all, what on earth was I supposed to do now?

Third breakfast seemed like a truly terrible idea and I knew Charles was busy at work, so after a few quick minutes to calm myself, I decided to call Nan.

"You say someone is threatening you on the Internet?" she asked as she frowned at me through the FaceTime app.

I nodded emphatically. "And I have no idea who or why."

Nan's expression softened, not just in sentiment but also because she had started messing with the beauty settings and filters on the app. "I wouldn't worry about it too much, dear. They probably just have you confused for somebody else," she assured me as rainbow unicorns danced over her head in the frame.

"Maybe," I agreed while picking at the skin on my elbow to calm my nerves.

"Just try to relax and enjoy your day," my grandmother suggested from beneath a sky of twinkling pink stars. "Grant and I are catching a matinee, but I'll see you after for tea?"

"Yeah, sure." My throat was dry and my voice sounded terrible, but I was a grown woman. I needed to learn how to solve some problems on my own.

And this was a doozy.

Charm could very well be some rando just messing with me for fun, or they could be an enemy fully intent on ruining my life. I'd sent more than one person to prison in my days as an investigator. Maybe one of them had been released and was now looking for revenge. In any case, it wouldn't hurt to do a bit of research on their whereabouts.

I grabbed a pad of sticky notes out of the top drawer of my desk and wrote down the first bad guy I'd helped catch—my former friend, Diane Fulton. We'd been pretty close back when I worked at the law firm, but that hadn't stopped her from trying to kill me when I found out the truth about what happened to Octo-Cat's previous owner, how *she* was the one at fault.

I tore off the sticky and attached it to my desk then returned my attention to the pad. Enemy number two was a realtor from Misty Harbor,

Sandra Lyn. She was responsible for a double homicide and had almost let an innocent man endure life in prison at her expense. It seemed unlikely she'd be out of the cage or have access to social media within it, but I would still need to do a bit of research before crossing her off my list. I placed her name next to Diane's.

My third enemy was my former boss, Richard Thompson. He'd murdered my former neighbor, a beloved senator with a soft spot for protecting the environment. To add insult to injury, my cat had peed on him while the cops had him restrained on the ground.

I tore off the sticky note and added it to the growing collection on my desk. *Hoo, boy.* Despite being out of work for most of my career as a P.I., I had sure managed to amass quite the list of enemies—and I was only just getting started with my task of enumerating them all.

I paused to shake my hand out before racking my brain for the next suspect. Considering my ads were geo-targeted, I should probably be looking specifically for someone who was still residing within the Blueberry Bay area, right?

No, I probably shouldn't rule anybody out. The sooner I uncovered Charm's secret identity, the sooner I could get back to my very full schedule of... nothing.

Sigh.

Well, at least I now had something to keep me busy.

Thanks, Charm.

3

"Whatcha doing?" Charlene, our little black kitten, jumped up onto my desk to investigate. At this point I had so many sticky notes, I'd recently started affixing them to the wall as well.

"Making a list of suspects," I answered distractedly as I scrawled *Sara Stevens* onto a hot pink Post-It and tore it from the pad.

Charlene moved to study the writing. "Suh," she sounded out slowly, then "ah," "ruh," and another "ah" as in *apple*.

"Sara," I supplied, then looked up at her with wide eyes. "Wait, are you learning to read?"

She plopped her rear onto the desk and lifted

her chin with pride. "Papa Octo-Cat is teaching me. He says I'm a very smart young lady."

I reached out to stroke her head and was met in turn by a rumbling, contented purr. "Charlene, that's fantastic."

"I want to be brilliant like Papa Octo-Cat when I grow up and beautiful like Mama Grizz," Charlene informed me as she leaned in to each stroke of my hand.

I laughed at that. Of course Octo-Cat referred to himself as *brilliant*. *Smart* just wasn't high enough praise. "Seems you're well on your way. What about your aunt and uncle? Do you want to be like them too?" I asked, referring to the Sphynxes who seemed to love Charlene every bit as much as her adoptive parents did.

"Auntie J and Uncle J are fun!" Charlene enthused while bobbing her head up and down.

Fun was not the word I'd use to describe the two hairless cats, but they'd only taken to me after a significant amount of hesitation and threats from Octo-Cat to really drive the point home.

"What are you learning from them in your lessons?" I asked, more curious now than when I'd first heard of their special homeschool arrangement.

The black kitten shook her head. "I'm not allowed to tell. Cat class is for cats only."

"But you told me you're learning to read?" I pointed out.

She scrunched her face up and thought about this for a moment before breaking out in a relieved smile and saying, "That's an extra-circular, so it's okay."

"An extra*curricular*?" I offered with a slight giggle. "Like outside of your normal studies?"

"Exactly. An extra-circle-ular."

I patted her head again. I knew Charlene had to grow up, but I hoped she would never change. Her pure joy and wonderment often helped me see the world through new eyes myself. I certainly felt better about investigating my online bully since she'd joined me in the office.

Charlene stuck around, keeping me company while I finished making my list and attempting to read each name as I placed it with the others.

"Your handwriting is very sloppy," she told me at one point, proof that Octo-Cat was, indeed, teaching her how to be a cat in every sense of the word.

Rather than scold her or defend myself, I let her remark slide, hoping the casual insult was a one-off. Besides, I was too distracted by the task at hand to jump into full-on lecture mode.

When I'd finished, I had a total of fourteen sticky notes with fourteen names—and no idea where to start.

The doorbell rang, announcing Nan's arrival.

"Coming!" I called at the top of my lungs, scooping Charlene into my arms and shutting the office door firmly behind me.

By the time I reached the top of the staircase, Nan had already let herself into the house and was shrugging out of her light windbreaker.

"Did you have a nice time out with Grant?" I asked and her cheeks immediately grew rosy.

"I'd forgotten how much I love being married," she admitted, fluffing her hair demurely then coming in for a hug once I had reached the bottom of the stairs and set Charlene onto the hardwood floor. The kitten immediately raced toward the kitchen, presumably in search of the other cats, leaving Nan and me to ourselves.

"Where's Paisley?" I asked, glancing around the foyer. Nan and I always had lots of animal company. It was strange that we didn't now.

"I came straight from the cinema," she informed me, unbothered by the absence of furry companions. "Grant dropped me off because you seemed so distressed when you called earlier."

"Distressed is putting it lightly," I admitted, chewing on my bottom lip as I thought back to those initial messages that had set me on edge.

"I'll put on the kettle while you catch me up on the finer details." Nan floated toward the kitchen, and I ran upstairs to grab my laptop.

"See," I said pointing at the screen once I'd pulled up the ad and its comments.

"You don't know me, but you do know what I'm talking about," my grandmother read aloud and then tutted. "What a rude individual this Charm is. Kind of ironic, don't you think?"

I didn't want to debate whether the username fit the user. I wanted to figure out who was on the other side of that screen. "Do you think they know my secret? Or what I can do?" I asked, hoping to refocus my nan.

"How would they? This is probably just some crazy person trying to get a rise out of you. The Internet is full of them, you know." She shook her head and said nothing more. Why wasn't she getting what a huge deal this whole thing was turning out to be? It could ruin my whole life if I wasn't careful, if I didn't act fast.

"I haven't always been as careful as I should," I argued, averting my gaze toward the floor. It physically pained me to think back over all the times I'd been careless with protecting my secret. Those times easily outnumbered my list of enemies at least a dozen to one.

And what if Charm wasn't an enemy at all? What if they were just some random person who had stumbled upon what I could do and was now trying to extort money from me?

"What do you think they want?" I asked Nan, glancing from her to the screen and back again.

Nan grabbed the computer from my hands. "Well, why don't we ask."

I watched as she typed in slow motion, one finger at a time: *What do you want?*

For as slow as Nan was, Charm's response came instantaneously: *I want the truth to come out.*

"Well, that's not good," Nan said as I stared at the threatening comment over her shoulder.

"Not good," she agreed with a slight shake of her head before turning to face me. "But not necessarily bad."

"How can this be anything but bad?" I whined.

"This Charm character probably doesn't know

anything. They're just trying to get a rise out of you."

"And if Charm actually knows my secret? Then what?" I demanded, taking the laptop back and hugging it to my chest.

"Then what's so bad about coming out with it? Talking to animals is a huge part of who you are. Why hide it?" Nan shrugged as if this recommendation was one I could actually take, as if my entire life weren't currently on the line.

"Do you not recall how it ruined Grandma Lyn's life?" I challenged with one eyebrow raised.

She simply shrugged again. "True, but people are more open minded these days."

"I don't want to become the punchline to some poorly told joke. I just want to live a normal life," I whined. I hated that I was whining or groaning all my words today but I couldn't help it given my current state of distress.

Nan blinked up at me with wide eyes, a sly smile blooming on her face. "My dear sweet Angela, when has your life ever been normal?"

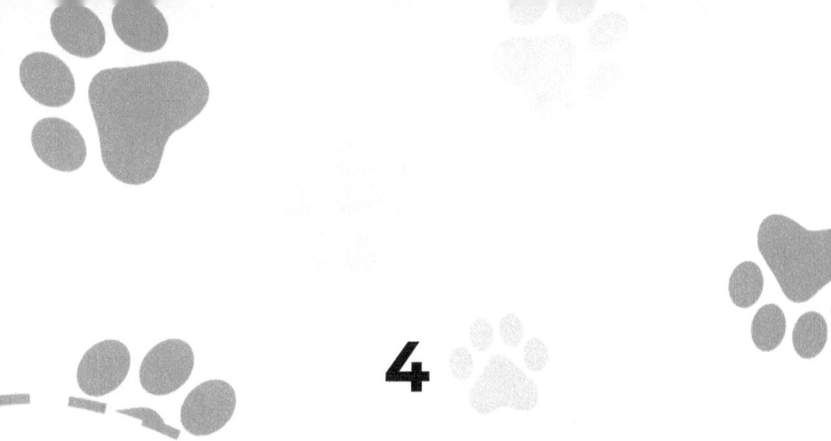

4

Whether or not Octo-Cat wanted anything more to do with the sleuthing business, he was still half owner of Pet Whisperer, P.I.—and I needed his help now more than ever.

After Nan left, I searched the house until I found him sitting in his bedroom watching the fish swim about his 140-gallon aquarium.

"Yummy is looking particularly plump today," he noted as I entered. "Maybe I'll just try a quick bite."

Of course, he'd named all his fish various synonyms of the word "delicious." I thought he did it mostly to get a rise out of me, since every time he hinted at eating his pets, I rushed to buy him fresh shrimp or his favorite lobster rolls from Little Dog Diner.

"Not today," I warned with a stern look.

That got his attention. "Keep your voice down. The child is sleeping." He motioned toward his red silk cat bed where Charlene was dozing tucked under a pillow that was almost as large as the bed itself.

"Can we go somewhere to talk?" I whispered, kneeling down to bring myself closer to his height. I locked eyes with him and then put every ounce of desperate passion into my next words. *"It's important."*

Octo-Cat abruptly turned away from me, speaking back over his shoulder. "I don't like your tone of voice today, Angela," the tabby complained. "Maybe we can talk once you've had a chance to gain control of your emotions?"

"I am not being emotional," I shouted and stamped my foot in frustration. "I am having the proper anxiety response to a very big, very new threat, and I'd feel better if I could just talk to you about it!"

Across the room, Charlene mewled and popped her head out from beneath the pillow. Oops, I'd forgotten the need to be quiet. Maybe I really was a touch emotional over everything that was going on. I wouldn't be nearly as perturbed if my business partner and supposed best friend would just listen to me.

"Now you've really done it," he growled and rushed to lick the head of his beloved adopted daughter. "There, there, sweet pea. Papa is here. The mean old lady was just leaving."

I refused to accept being called "old," and frankly, Octavius hadn't seen mean yet, but if he kept this song-and-dance up, he soon would.

"What's wrong?" Charlene asked me with a soft voice and wide golden eyes as Octo-Cat continued to snuggle her protectively.

For a moment, I considered how much I should reveal in front of the youngest member of our household. I didn't want to frighten her, yet I didn't want to hide any important truths from her either.

Ultimately, I decided to reveal everything and use gentle language to do so. I took a deep breath before launching into my slightly censored explanation. "Someone is sending me messages online, saying they know I can talk to animals, and they're going to tell everybody about it."

There. It really didn't sound nearly as bad when I put it that way.

Octo-Cat stared at me as he flicked his tail back and forth, presumably deep in thought. At least I hoped so, seeing as I could really use his perspective on this whole thing.

Charlene, however, spoke up immediately. "Who is saying those things to you?"

I forced myself to shrug nonchalantly. "I don't know. It's a mystery."

Charlene rose to her feet and stretched, shaking off her father's continued attentions. "Isn't that what you do best? Solve mysteries? You found my mother when she was missing and figured out who was hurting your mate, remember?"

Of course I remembered. All of that had happened just a couple weeks ago, but I refused to be snarky with a kitten, especially one who was just trying to help.

"You haven't been careful," Octo-Cat decided with a low rumbling in his throat that fell somewhere between a growl and a purr.

"I should have been more careful," I admitted. "But I can't go back and change the past, so how do we fix this in the here and now?"

"We could build a time machine!" Charlene cried, jumping into the air so that none of her four feet touched the ground. "That would fix every-thing!" she added once she'd landed.

"Time machines aren't real," I said with a soft chuckle as I reached out to stroke her fur.

"But Papa Octo-Cat said—"

Octo-Cat put a paw in front of his daughter's mouth. "Some knowledge is for cats only. You must never share what you learn during cat lessons," he said gravely.

"Not even with Angie?" the little one squeaked.

"Especially not with Angela. She already knows too much, as it is."

"Um, hello, I'm still here," I said, turning their attention back to me. Honestly, I didn't even want to know what they were yammering on about. Time machines? What ridiculous nonsense.

"Can we please redirect our attention to the problem at hand?" I begged, having completely discarded any lingering sense of pride long ago when it came to this situation.

"But I was—" Charlene began, but stopped abruptly when Octo-Cat shook his head.

"Proceed," the elder feline said with a wave of his paw in my direction.

"The person threatening me goes by the name of Charm. Really, they could be anybody, but I thought we could start by going over a list of suspects I made."

"All the pretty papers with words!" Charlene cried, all the pieces finally clicking into place for her. "You said that was a list of suspects."

"Yes, that was my list of suspects, and it includes anyone whose nefarious plans we've thwarted over the years. Unfortunately, it is not a short list."

"So what do you want me to do about it?" Octo-Cat asked with another flick of his tail.

My heart dropped. He knew how important maintaining my secret was to me. Did he really not care? "Help me," I enunciated slowly before adding, "You are my partner, after all."

He sighed and shook his head. "I told you, I'm a family man now. I don't have time to go on any more wild goose chases with you, Angela, especially not any that could be dangerous."

"But Octavius, this isn't just some throw-away case. This is my life." I brought my hands together in supplication, praying the haughty kitty would take pity on me and agree to lend his brain to the investigation. *"Please. Octo-Cat, I need you."*

Octo-Cat remained silent, but it seemed my

appeal had gotten through to at least one of the cats.

"We've got to help her, Papa," Charlene insisted, coming up to me and rubbing her body against my arm. Moving to Octo-Cat, she did the same, claiming him with a friendly snuggle. "She helped me when I was scared and lost, and look how sad she is!"

I pouted my lower lip and made my eyes extra wide to drive home the kitten's point.

Charlene and I both stared at Octo-Cat, knowing that he needed to be the next to say something.

After several tense moments passed, he finally let out a long sigh and said, "this is the last time." His stony gaze fixed on mine as he added, "The very last time. I mean it."

"Thank you," I mouthed, overcome with a tremendous sense of relief.

If I couldn't turn the business around, this would be the last time, regardless. And if by some miracle I managed to save us, then I could worry about convincing Octo-Cat when the time came to take on our next case.

Either way, I needed to get to the bottom of this

whole Charm thing before they made a mockery of both the business and my life.

5

"So we're assuming Charm is a human, correct?" Octo-Cat asked after reviewing my hastily scrawled Post-It note suspects. And honestly I hadn't even considered that it might be an animal messing with me, until he suggested otherwise. How would an animal even be capable of typing out those messages—and so quickly? Then again, what if I overlooked the true identity based on making sweeping assumptions like that?

"Uh..." I really didn't know how to answer him. Luckily, Octo-Cat had much more to say on the subject.

"A cat is above all this," he pointed out drolly. "And a dog isn't smart enough. Wild animals wouldn't have access to the Internet. That leaves humans."

"Fair point," I conceded with a nod. Was it really that easy? See, this was why I needed him.

"I also think you can cross any murderers off your list." He pawed at the note with Diane Fulton's name scrawled across it, wrinkling his nose in disgust. "Why would they stoop to making idle threats when they've killed before? If they truly wanted revenge, Angela, they'd just off you."

"That's... not a comforting thought," I murmured as my heart sped to a gallop in my chest. My throat also seemed to be closing in on itself. Maybe my cat was right; maybe Charm wasn't a murderer, but did that mean there might actually be someone else out there plotting my demise?

"It's a good argument, though." Octo-Cat turned his nose up, oblivious to the effect his candor was having on my mental health.

"Do you think Charm is someone we've interacted with more recently?" I asked next. The sooner we narrowed down our list, the sooner I could start investigating each lead. "I mean, why would Anne Fulton, for example, come out of the woodwork now?"

Octo-Cat shuddered. "Don't ever speak that

name in my presence again." Anne was the one who had kidnapped him and held him for ransom in a last-ditch effort to contest the will that left him almost everything. It made sense that he didn't have fond memories of her. Then again, that's how I felt about basically every single name under consideration.

"I don't really know," Octo-Cat confessed, resettling himself on the desk. He'd taken Charlene back to the Sphynx cats for kitten-sitting while we worked on our newest mystery, but I could tell he was eager to return to his charge. "It could very well be someone you haven't even thought of yet."

I sighed and leaned back in my chair. "That's what I'm afraid of. Until I figure out who Charm is, I can't really trust anyone."

Octo-Cat sneered at me. "I'd be careful about making such general statements. You can trust me, Charlene, Charles, Nan…"

I raised an eyebrow in interest. "You didn't mention Jacques and Jillianne."

"I still haven't forgiven the exhibitionists for the mess they caused at our wedding." A light growl sounded in his throat at the memory.

"I don't think they're behind this, though," I said softly, not wanting to create drama where there needn't be any. "Everyone's been getting along so well lately."

Octo-Cat sighed and nodded his head in concession. "And I remain convinced a human is to blame this time, so we should probably cross them off the list anyway."

"Maybe we can make a second list, one for everyone who already knows my secret?" I groaned and reached for my sticky pads again. "At least it will be shorter than my list of enemies."

"Remember that weird author we met on our road trip? Melissa something?" Octo-Cat said, his eyes closed up tight while he thought. "She knew because Nan had been blabbing to her friends on the Internet."

Dread roiled in my gut. "You're right. There's no telling how many people found out that way. But that was more than a year ago. Ever since Nan and I had our talk, she's stopped gossiping on online message boards. She even removed all her old posts."

"So?" the cat challenged, opening his eyes again to stare at me coldly.

"So it doesn't make sense for one of those people to be messing with me now. Too much time has passed." Right? Right? That had to be the case.

"What if that person suddenly needs money or a favor?" Octo-Cat raised both whiskered eyebrows. "Maybe they hadn't needed to threaten you before, but desperate times and all that."

"So our suspect list is every human with the Internet?" I glanced at my desk with trepidation. I didn't have anywhere near enough Post-It notes—or wall space—for that.

One of Octo-Cat's fangs came out to rest on his lower lip, giving him a comical appearance. His words, however, were anything but. "Well, as you pointed out, it's been a long time. Even people without Internet may still have come into contact with the info by other means."

"Which means our suspect list is every human in the entire world?" God help me, I didn't have the strength for this.

Octo-Cat nodded. "Every living human."

I groaned and threw the notepad down onto my desk. "This isn't helping."

"You're the one who's forcing me to be here," my cat challenged.

"Fine, then go," I barked out, trying not to let any tears spill from my burning eyes.

Octo-Cat rose to his feet, but paused to study me. "It's going to be okay, Angela," he offered as parting words. "One way or another, it will all work itself out. But if Charm doesn't want us to know their identity, I don't see how we're going to figure it out. Maybe you should stop trying to figure out who they are and instead start focusing on what you're going to do once your secret comes out."

"Please just go," I said between clenched teeth. He was already assuming I would fail. I didn't need that. Couldn't handle it, either.

I kept my head bowed toward my lap as I struggled to work through my emotions. By the time I raised my eyes again to glance around the room, my cat had gone. It was times like this I really missed Paisley and her eternal optimism. I knew Octo-Cat was being a realist here, but I also needed to live in my secret fantasy world just a little bit longer—especially if Charm was going to come and pull the rug out from under my feet any second now.

If Octo-Cat wouldn't help me and Nan refused to see the problem, that meant I had to find someone else to confide in. Of course, I knew Grandma Lyn would be a good person to go to. She could talk to animals too, but when she tried to share her secret with her husband at the time, he not only left her, he stole her baby away too. Being honest about what she could do ruined her life.

Sure, times had changed and my husband already knew and accepted all parts of me—including this one—but what if something awful still happened as a result of Charm outing me?

Octo-Cat said that if my bully didn't want me to know their identity, then there was no way I'd be able to figure it out. But he was an amateur on social media... at best.

And while I myself wasn't the greatest, I did have someone else I could turn to—someone who not only understood the intricate ins and outs of the Interweb but also made a living at it.

Yes, I decided. My cousin Mags would know what to do, and it was just about time I gave her a call.

6

grabbed my laptop and headed upstairs to the tower bedroom that Charles and I now shared.

Crossing my legs beneath me, I opened the computer and messaged Mags an *SOS*.

Almost as soon as I pressed send, my phone buzzed beside me. "Hello?"

"What's the emergency? How can I help?" my cousin asked breathlessly, leaving me to wonder if she had just stopped a workout on my account.

Well, might as well just come straight out with it. "Someone's threatening me online, and I was hoping you could help me figure out who."

Mags's breathing slowed to a more measured pace. "Oooh, a bit of digital sleuthing? I'm in, although I definitely don't like that someone's picking on you. How bad is it?"

I closed my eyes to hold in the tears. "They say they know what I can do, and they're going to tell everyone."

Mags took a long, slow breath on the other end of the line. "Okay, okay, that could mean anything."

"Yeah, but we both know what it *does* mean. Are you near your computer? I can do a screen share, so you can see everything."

"I can be in five minutes," my cousin promised. "Want me to stay on with you until I get home?"

"Yes, please." Hearing her voice brought a much-needed smile to my face, and I wasn't willing to let that go just yet—not even for a single second.

While Mags power-walked back to her house, I filled her in on the details I had so far as well as some of my guesses for who might be behind Charm's messages.

"I'm home now. Just booting my PC. Shoot me a Zoom link on messenger."

I dutifully did as requested and waited for Mags to join the meeting room before we hung up on the phone and switched to this new means of communication.

A moment later, Mags's face appeared bright

and rosy; her hair hung in a loose ponytail at the nape of her neck.

"I didn't mean to interrupt your exercise," I said, feeling bad about how little I actually worked out myself.

Mags shook her head and waved her hands in front of the camera. "But this can't wait. I'm glad you called me. Now, show me the comments."

I shared my computer screen and navigated back toward the ad, so Mags could see everything for herself.

"Hmmm," was all she said.

"Is that a good hmm or a bad hmm?"

"Right now it's a curious hmm. Click on the profile."

I watched the tiny window with Mags's video feed as she leaned forward and squinted. And once again I did as instructed. Charm's profile was still locked due to their high-level privacy settings.

Mags groaned when she saw that. "They're giving us nothing. Not even a location."

"Well, it has to be someone local, right? Otherwise they wouldn't have seen my ad. I only targeted people within a twenty-five mile radius." I still felt proud that I'd figured the ads thing out all by myself. Not that they'd brought me any clients, but still.

"Actually..." Mags shared her screen, which in turn minimized mine. I watched eagerly as she clicked around on my page and then brought up the same ad where Charm was leaving nasty comments. "See, anyone can find your ads if they know where to look."

"So we're back to my suspect list being basically everyone on planet Earth," I ground out in defeat.

Mags's blonde brows pinched together in confusion. "What?"

I waved a hand dismissively. "Just something Octo-Cat was saying."

"Okay, well..." Mags stopped sharing her computer screen, and her flushed face once again filled the picture window. "You made a list of your enemies, right?"

I nodded.

"And a list of everyone who already knows your secret?"

"Well, I started to, but then Octo-Cat pointed out that Nan had been pretty free about sharing my secret online about a year ago. Those posts are gone now, but anyone could have seen them while they were still up."

Mags shook her head, then said, "Hmm. That's a me-feeling-bad-for-you hmm by the way."

"Thanks" was all I could manage to say in response. At least I had her sympathy, if nothing else.

We sat in silence for a few beats before Mags's face lit up anew. "Okay, here's what we do. So far we've been focused on brainstorming who you know that might say these things based on your past encounters. But we shouldn't be focusing on the past."

This admittedly confused me. "We shouldn't?" As a private investigator, focusing on the past was all I did as I tried to piece together what happened and save the day.

But Mags was insistent. "No, we need to focus on the here and now. We don't have much on Charm, but everything we do have is a clue."

"I'm listening." I moved my hands to my lap to avoid fidgeting while she explained.

"Go back to Charm's page and enlarge that profile picture," my cousin commanded, staring intently at the screen.

Once we'd returned to the profile, we both stared at the photo of a tranquil ocean. I, for one, had no ideas.

"Okay, so I just did a quick reverse image search, and nothing is coming up. Or rather, too much is coming up. The photo is too generic to match, which means that could be any ocean anywhere," Mags explained, her shoulders slumping. Was she also ready to admit defeat, just like Octo-Cat?

"Do you think Charm lives by the ocean?" I prompted, still unwilling to let her go.

"I have no idea. I was hoping I'd find something, but no such luck." She shook her head before pointing at me in the screen. "But there's still more we can look at. Their comments—what they say and how they say things."

"So far there hasn't been anything that stands out. At least not to me."

"Me neither, but maybe we can trick Charm into revealing himself—or herself."

"Should I ask them a question?" I waited, hands poised over the keyboard.

"I'm thinking of the right way to word it. Unfortunately, since their profile is set to private, the only way for you to reach out is very publicly through that ad. We have to be very careful about how we proceed."

I blinked hard. Everything about this made me

super nervous, but what other choice did I have? At least Mags was ready and able to help.

Mags sat straight again, her face glowed with the promise of a new idea. "Oh, I've got it. Type this."

I wrote out Mags's response word for word: *Let's meet to discuss this. How about the Little Dog Diner tonight at five?*

"Good thinking," I enthused as a wave of relief rushed over me. "That will help determine if Charm is local."

"And if they're willing to put their money where their mouth is," I added.

"Exactly?" Mags bobbed her head before suddenly pausing to ask, "What money? What mouth?"

I laughed at that. "Sometimes you're as bad as the cats. You know that?"

Mags blew a raspberry at me. "Hey, you're the one with all the fancy idioms. Not me."

Mags and I chatted back and forth as we waited for a response, but ultimately none came. I glanced at the time in the corner of my computer screen and sighed.

"Guess I better get ready to head out. Thanks for all your help, Mags."

"Keep me posted," my cousin cried before her face disappeared from the screen, leaving me completely and utterly alone.

Now that the moment was nigh, I found myself equal parts excited and terrified. Was I really on the way to meet my accuser? Could this really all be over before my husband even made it home from work?

Oh, how I hoped so.

7

I sent Charles a quick text to let him know I would be picking up lobster rolls for dinner, then hopped behind the steering wheel and began the long drive to Misty Harbor.

As I navigated the streets of the area I'd called home my entire life, I began to wonder how any of the friendly people here could want to ruin me. True, we had our fair share of murderers and other con artists, but I'd only ever tried to help people—to put good out into the world.

And now someone was threatening to bring that to an end once and for all.

Was I endangering myself by meeting with this person face-to-face? By asking to talk about things, I was also all but confirming whatever they believed to be true. What were the chances they'd been hinting at something completely unrelated to my ability to talk to animals? What if they actually assumed something far worse about me?

Nope. I did not like this situation one bit.

At least Mags took my concern seriously, but it hurt that Nan and Octo-Cat both remained largely unbothered. And, yeah, I probably should have told Charles by now, but he was so busy at work, making up for all the time he took off for our honeymoon.

I'd tell him tonight, though, over our favorite meal from our favorite diner to soften the blow.

These swirling thoughts of fear, self-doubt, and indecision kept my mind busy until I reached my destination.

When I entered my beloved diner, the waitress on duty caught sight of me immediately. "Four lobster rolls to go, darling?" she asked with a huge smile as she wiped down menus with a wet cloth. She was newer and I couldn't quite remember her name, but she definitely knew me and my order.

"Actually..." I coughed into my fist, suddenly very nervous. What if Charm was already here? What if they were watching me right now? I desperately glanced around the establishment as my pulse pounded in my ears.

"Actually?" the waitress prompted with a reassuring nod when I didn't immediately continue.

My eyes zoomed back to hers, and I jammed both hands into my pockets to hide that they were shaking. "I'd like to stick around for a little while before I grab those rolls to go. May I have a table? And a Diet Coke?"

"You've got it, babe. Sit anywhere you'd like. I'll be right with you." She seemed relieved to bring our awkward exchange to an end—or at least to put it on hold.

Once I was seated, I glanced around the other patrons of the diner a second time. Almost everyone was closer to Nan's age than my own. Did I really think that sweet old man wearing coke bottle glasses and polka-dotted suspenders was capable of Charm's heinous behavior?

The waitress brought me my soda, and I sucked it down while continuing to catalog the other diners. No one paid me any mind, except to smile politely or give a quick nod of acknowledgment.

None were Charm. I was sure of it.

"Waiting for someone?" the waitress asked

kindly after stopping at a nearby table to distribute entrees.

"Yeah," I said, my voice suddenly hoarse.

"If they'll be here soon, I can put in an order," she offered with a grin. "Or I can at least bring you a refill on your Diet Coke."

How long did I want to commit to waiting for someone who might never show, someone I was less and less sure I actually wanted to meet as time droned on?

"Um, I'm actually not sure when they'll be here. Let me just check my phone." I smiled awkwardly at the waitress as she waited, tray held high. With shaking fingers, I scrolled to the ad where all my interactions with Charm had taken place.

Nothing.

This was stupid. I had no reason to believe they were actually coming. I should have stayed at home rather than driving all the way out here. And yet, I just so desperately wanted the whole thing to be over.

Well, we can't always get what we want, I supposed.

"Everything okay?" the waitress asked, lowering her tray and tilting her head to the side.

"I'll take those lobster rolls to go now," I answered with a forced smile.

"Be back in a jiff," she assured me before floating off toward the back kitchen.

I nodded, but I just couldn't tear my eyes away from the phone's tiny screen. Even though I knew better, I couldn't help but type out a new reply: *You're not here.*

This time Charm responded promptly: *I never said I was coming. Someone seems pretty desperate to meet up though.*

After the words, Charm posted three skull emojis.

What was *that* supposed to mean?

I decided to send a quick screenshot to Mags and ask her.

Dead came her immediately reply. *Likely dead laughing. They're making fun of you.*

I bristled. Glad this was all one big joke to Charm. Meanwhile, my entire day had been spoiled, and I was still no closer to figuring out who they were or what they really wanted.

A few minutes later, the waitress set a white paper bag down before me. "Tada, four lobster rolls to go!"

Oops. I'd forgotten to modify my usual order to

reflect the current members of our household, but I also had no guarantee that Charlene, Jacque, or Jillianne would even like the food. It was weird enough that Octo-Cat did.

I handed the waitress a wad of cash, thanked her for the help, and then bolted out that door. No one there knew what was going on, but I was still thoroughly embarrassed by the ordeal.

It all felt so hopeless.

I felt hopeless.

I'd barely gotten back in my car when my phone rang. I let the Bluetooth route the call through my speakers, and Charles's voice wrapped around me like a warm hug.

"I'm home, but where is my beautiful bride?" he wanted to know.

"I'm about thirty minutes away," I said, checking the GPS for an ETA. True, I knew this area like the back of my hand, but sometimes I got so wrapped up in my inner thoughts that I missed my turn-off.

"You sound…" My husband started but then abruptly switched gears. "Everything okay?"

"It's been a day," I admitted with a sigh. "I don't want to trouble you with it." I don't know why I said that. It wasn't true at all. I very much needed someone on my side, someone who wasn't a thousand miles away like Mags.

"Hey, I knew what I signed on for when we said 'I do.' Half your problems are now my problems, so let's hear it. Maybe I can help."

It was then I finally began to cry. I cried so hard I had to pull over on the side of the road until my vision cleared enough to continue the drive. And I told Charles everything right from that first introduction to Charm all the way down to the row of skull emojis and everything in between.

"Honey, honey, it's okay," he said. Charles had taken to the nickname after the whole fiasco with the bees on our honeymoon. "We'll figure it out together. If nothing else, I can send a cease and desist. That often scares people enough to make them stop whatever it is they're doing."

I let out a long, shaky breath. "Yeah, okay."

"I wish you would have called me when this first started."

"But you're busy with work. I didn't want to distract you," I argued, at the same time regretting that I hadn't. Charles always knew just what to do, no matter how big the problem.

"Work is work, but Angie, you're my whole life."

"I love you," I said with another sob.

"I love you too, but..." His voice switched from soft to stern in an instant. "I don't love that you tried to meet this person by yourself. That could have been really dangerous."

"I know," I confessed. I deserved his ire, there was no denying that. "I was just so desperate for it to be over."

"Leave it with me," he said decisively. "Do you mind if I use your laptop? I have some questions for this Charm."

"Have at it," I said, then blew my nose loudly in a tissue.

"Drive safe," was the last thing Charles said before ending the call, and then I was alone again.

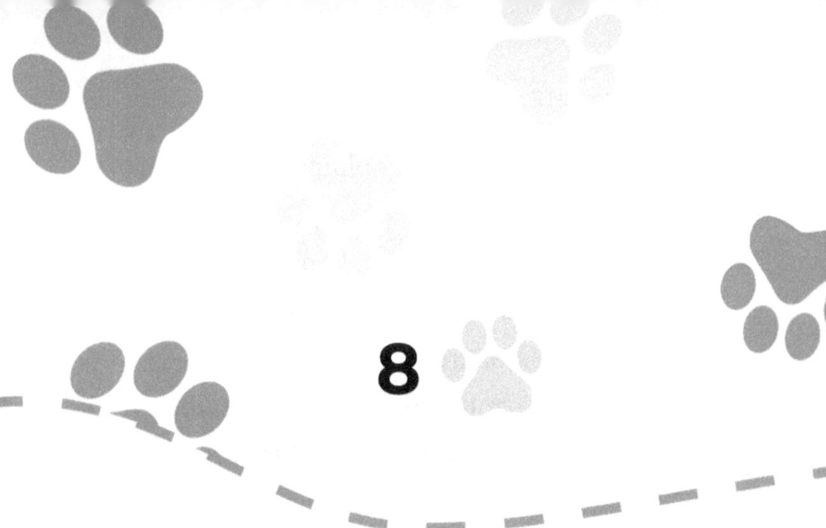

8

Thirty minutes later, I marched through the front door, lobster rolls held out in front of me like some kind of sacred offering.

"Finally," my cat yowled, jumping from the bottom step of the grand staircase and trotting briskly toward the dining room.

"What do you mean *finally*? You didn't even know I was going out!" I huffed.

The only response was the jaunty swish of Octo-Cat's tail as he departed.

"Is that my wifey?" Charles's voice sounded from above.

I turned back toward the staircase and watched

him race down the steps, holding on to my laptop with a tight grip.

I was almost afraid to ask. "Any luck?"

The corners of Charles's mouth tilted down as he revealed, "It's Blaire."

"Blaire," I parroted in bewilderment, then it hit me. "Blaire from-our-honeymoon Blaire?"

"Look at this." Charles motioned me to join him at the table, then set the laptop before us and pressed play on a video I'd never seen before.

In it, I stood in a beautiful garden having a conversation with a queen bee named Bey. That whole scene had played out sometime between two and three weeks ago at our honeymoon in Virginia. The recording only showed my side of the conversation. I guess Bey's quiet buzzy voice just couldn't be captured on film.

"Aldrin and Lightyear told me about the over-harvesting and the new plants," my likeness said. The camera wasn't particularly close, but you could still see the hint of a sympathetic expression on my face.

Video-me paused while Bey responded, and the person taking the video attempted to zoom in on the queen bee who sat perched upon a flower. I only knew she was there because I'd been there too. For viewers, she was much too small to see.

"This garden has sentimental value," my recorded self continued. "I can understand that. What can I do to help ensure you can stay?"

The camera panned out, bringing me back into frame.

"Oh, yes, that reminds me, please don't sting my husband. He is a good man, and very allergic."

Another long pause.

"While I have you, then, have you noticed any other strange goings-on in this garden or its house?"

The video cut off abruptly even though I knew the conversation continued for some time after that.

"Well, that isn't so bad, right? I mean, you can't even tell who I'm talking to, really. Nobody will accept this as any real kind of proof," I argued, waiting for my husband to agree.

He did not.

"Yeah, but then there's this one too," Charles informed me, clicking on a second video while I was still trying to process the first. Now I sat inside cross-legged on the floor as I visited with Charlene and her mother cat, the one we'd worked so hard to find during our trip. That was our last day in Virginia before we headed home with the kitten in tow. I remembered it vividly. I had asked Blaire for some privacy while I said goodbye. The rainbow-haired girl had adopted the mother cat and named her Socks, despite the fact that Socks was a tortie with not a drop of white on her.

Blaire had left us alone then, but must have set up a secret camera somewhere first. She already knew what I could do since the conversation with Queen Bey had happened days earlier. I should have known better, too. I'd caught her recording when Charles fell through the staircase, and it was her secret recording of a midnight meeting between Mrs. MacKenzie and Billy that had revealed the true culprits behind everything that had gone wrong at the inn. Blaire always had that phone in her hands, and she was always recording. Of course she'd recorded me. Of course she had. And yet...

I let out a long sigh. "I don't get it. We helped that girl. We arranged for that job and a place to live. Why would she suddenly blackmail me like this?"

"Why don't you ask her directly?" Charles suggested, tilting the laptop toward me on the table.

"I asked her to private message the page, by the way. None of those videos were posted publicly as far as I know."

Well, that was a relief, but it's the only thing that was. Now that I knew Charm's secret identity, I felt even worse. I'd never hurt her in any way. She had no reason to threaten me like this.

My fingers hovered over the keyboard as I thought of what to say. I decided to just be direct:

Blaire, why are you doing this?

Her response came rather unexpected. *Don't you want to be famous?*

"No!" I shouted at the computer, leading Charles to place his arms over my shoulder in support. "This is ridiculous."

"Just talk to her. It's the best chance you have of putting an end to all of this."

I want to live a normal life. What will it take to convince you to delete your videos and leave me alone?

"Even if she deletes the original videos, they're still probably backed up to the Cloud," Charles reminded me gently, proving I would never be safe even if I got Blaire to agree to silence.

What Blaire said next seemed to suggest we were having two different conversations.

Think of it. Endorsement deals. Reality shows. You could even become a TikTok influencer. And I'll manage the whole thing. For a cut.

She punctuated this with three wide eye emojis. The skull emojis from earlier probably should have clued me in that my bully was a member of Gen Z. A Millennial like myself would have used the cry-laughing emojis in that situation.

But I don't want any of that, I typed back furiously, then watched Charm's ocean profile pic bounce up and down as she typed. *Look, I'm offering you a chance to get in on the ground floor here. I already have the footage. It's mine to do what I want with.*

"Give me that," Charles said, practically tearing the computer away from me.

"Actually," he said every word aloud as he typed it into the chat. "Sharing these videos without Angie's consent is illegal. At best, it's an invasion of privacy. At worst, if you use the videos to garner endorsement deals or even just to monetize your feed, you're violating Angie's right of publicity, which is an even more serious charge. Is your address still the same? I need to know where to send the cease and desist letter."

I gave Charles an excited high five. Gosh, I loved

being married to an attorney. He always knew just how to scare people into compliance.

There was a long pause before Blaire started working on her response, and then: *Ah, you must be the "husband." Well, tell our girl that I was just trying to help her, but if she wants to be a wet blanket, that's on her. Stay poor for all I care.*

I let out a frustrated groan. "But we're not—"

Charles placed his hand on my shoulder and squeezed. "Don't say anything more. She should be done bothering you now. Just in case, we'll grab screenshots of this conversation and her comments on the ad."

It was true that Blaire knew Charles could get results. That was what had saved the inn back in Virginia and gotten her that job in the first place. I just couldn't believe she would throw it all back in our faces by trying to force me into some warped celebrity status so she could collect a side income. *Gross.*

I closed the laptop and turned toward my wonderful husband. "So what now?" I asked; already my heart was slowing back to its usual pace. My breath was coming easier, too.

But not everyone was relieved in that moment.

"For the love of all things fluffy," Octo-Cat

shouted at top volume. "Is anyone going to feed me?"

I laughed as I unwrapped a lobster roll for each of us.

And that first decadent bite? It tasted just like victory.

9

Charles and I had a great evening snuggling with the cats as we caught up on our Netflix to-watch list. I always felt so much better when he was home with me.

"I'm sorry I've been so busy with work lately," he mumbled when we were both brushing our teeth before bed. "There's been a rush of cases lately, but not enough to justify bringing on another attorney. You just never know what you'll get with small towns. There's either too much work or not enough."

Honestly I couldn't ever remember his workload falling under the "not enough" umbrella. Lately, though, it had risen to a whole new level. I was proud of my husband and his successful career, but

I also sometimes wanted to hide him away from the rest of the world so that he could be just mine, even if just for a few hours.

I finished brushing, spit my toothpaste foam into the sink, and gave Charles a peck on the cheek. "It's okay. I understand. I just miss you."

He leaned into my kiss for a moment before returning to his nightly ministrations. "I miss you too, honey. I love my job, but I wish I didn't have to work so much. I feel like I'm always missing out on things at home. Like this whole thing with Blaire..." He shook his head. "I should have been here."

"Seriously, don't worry about it. Today was an anomaly. Not much happens otherwise."

Charles glanced up to study my reflection in the bathroom mirror. "Are you sure you're okay?"

"I'm fine, or at least I will be. Just a lot of changes. Good changes, but they still take getting used to, you know?" I shrugged and applied some moisturizer to my face. Normally I didn't put any on at night, but I needed to keep my hands and mind busy as we chatted.

More than anything, I missed Charles, and I missed Nan. Sure I still saw both of them every day, but it just wasn't enough. I hated being on my own, and it so often felt like I was. Even Octo-Cat kept himself busy apart from me, considering he now had his daughter to look after. And I missed him, too.

God help me, I missed having my cranky cat criticize me! I was seriously starting to lose it here.

I needed to get my life figured out—and soon.

Unable to shut off my brain, I lay awake that night, lost in my thoughts while Charles dozed beside me. Maybe I could go out looking for mysteries to solve. While it would be great to make my business successful, more than anything I just needed something to keep me busy, to reignite that passion within me.

Feeling somewhat satisfied with my plan to roam the downtown area the next day, I at last fell into a fitful sleep. And by the time I awoke the next morning, Charles had already left for the office.

Bored, so bored.

And yet I had no energy to get ready and drag my sorry butt into town. It didn't really matter if I wore pajamas all day, did it? Or whether I brushed my hair?

It was funny that having nothing to do somehow made me want to do even less with myself. But I had no one to impress, so what did it even matter?

I puttered around on the computer for a while, mostly playing match-four games instead of actually doing anything that resembled work. Hmm. Maybe I should go back to school. Get another associate degree, or even go for my bachelor's. I'd always liked school. That's why I'd done so much of it.

Hey, maybe I could sneak into Charlene's cat lessons. Yeah, that would be something to do, and then I wouldn't be alone all day.

My mind made up, I shut down my computer and then slowly padded around the house in search of my feline roommates. It didn't take me long to discover that the Sphynxes had claimed Nan's old bedroom as their own, and that's where they'd created the makeshift classroom for their pupil.

I cracked the door and gave a listen: "If you have two dead mice but only one is really, truly dead, how should you reduce your treat intake to prevent flabbiness?" Jillianne asked in a rhythmic, lilting voice so unlike the one she used with me.

"Trick question!" the kitten cried in response. "Treat intake should never be reduced. Besides, I got lots of good exercise hunting those mice!"

"Very good!" the professorial cat mused. "Now if you'll—

Her voice dropped off at once as she spotted me in the doorway. "May I help you?"

Drats! I hadn't understood their odd mix of nutrition and algebra, but I had found it quite entertaining. "Sorry," I blurted out, opening the door the rest of the way and stepping into the room. Immediately, I noticed an odd collection of objects laid out on the bed between the cats: missing socks, trash, plants from outside, and some kind of furry carcass.

"No humans allowed," Jacques, the smaller of the two hairless cats, shouted, marching right up to me and then taking a swipe at my ankle. "Cat classes are for cats only. Now out! Shoo!"

"I don't mind if she stays," Charlene argued but was quickly overruled by her elders.

"What happens in cat school must stay in cat school," Jillianne decreed as her brother pushed me back into the hall.

Well, so much for that idea.

After that failed attempt at educating myself in the ways of catdom, I decided to go outside and take a walk about the property.

I'd barely managed to step off the porch before Pringle discovered me and quickly scampered over.

"Are we having story time early today?" the raccoon asked, rubbing his hands together like some kind of furry addict. "I can't wait to see how Merlin is going to defeat that mean, old ghost."

And because it was as good an idea as any, I nodded. "Sure, let's spend some time with Merlin, Gracie, and the gang."

Pringle leapt into the air with great vigor. He'd come so far since our first meeting, and it wasn't until very recently that I'd come to acknowledge his personal growth. If Octo-Cat didn't want to help with Pet Whisperer anymore, I knew Pringle would happily take over the role.

But was that what I wanted?

This gave me something to think on later, but for now, I'd lose myself in the magical mysteries of our favorite book series. I could figure out the mystery of my life later.

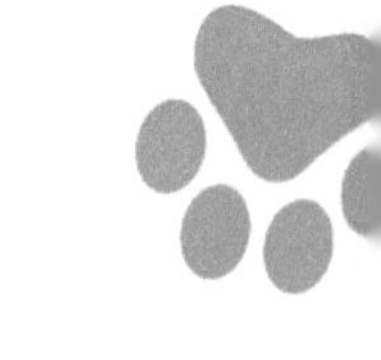

10

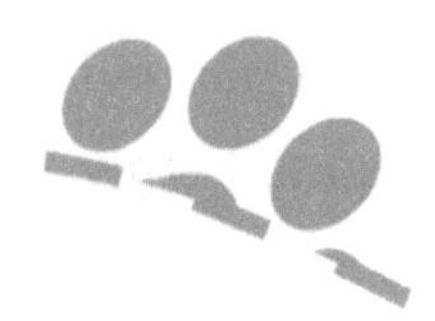

By the time Nan and Paisley turned up for lunch, I was beside myself with boredom and frustration. Octo-Cat had showed up unbidden at one point to give me a lecture about my intrusion upon Charlene's cat lessons, even going so far as to claim my innocent curiosity could disrupt the entire balance of the universe.

Yeah, sure. Sometimes my cat's inflated sense of self really wore on me. And sometimes it made me thankful that he kept busy parenting Charlene instead of constantly nagging me.

At least I had Nan and Paisley for a couple hours nearly every day to break up the monotony of my new life.

"I missed you so much!" Paisley cried out, wagging not just her tail, but her whole body as she slathered me in kisses and provided quite the contrast to my cat's attitude about me. It had only been one day since I last saw the good-natured Chihuahua, but I had felt her absence quite keenly during that time.

I scratched behind both of her ears and smiled. "I missed you too, baby dog." Then looking up at my grandmother asked, "How was your morning, Nan?"

She sashayed past, carrying two very full looking reusable grocery bags straight to the kitchen and calling out her answer as she went. "Grant and I started doing Tai Chi in the park downtown with some other seniors. This morning we were already there and halfway through our workout by the time the sun rose. It was magnificent."

Sounded like torture to me.

Nan poked her head through the kitchen doorway and smiled. "Are you sure you don't want to come along?"

"Nan, I'd be the youngest by at least forty years." I groaned as I drifted into the kitchen with Paisley scampering closely behind.

"So what's the big deal about that?"

While it was true I needed to find my place, I doubted that was with a group of health-nut octogenarians, and before sunrise at that. This was Nan's thing. I needed something that was all my own, another reason I so desperately wanted to turn Pet Whisperer P.I. around.

When my only response was an uncomfortable grimace, Nan waved her hand and returned her attention to the baking supplies. "Today I thought I could teach you how to make my famous blueberry scones," she explained as she unpacked first one bag and then the other. It looked as if she'd brought half the spice aisle with her.

"I was thinking about maybe going back to school," I mumbled, just to see how the idea might be received. I already knew I made a hopeless baker, which made it hard to pay attention. I had a lot of mental baggage I still needed to unload, too.

Nan paused and turned very slowly to look at me. "But you love being a detective. And you're so good at it."

I shrugged, attempting to appear nonchalant. "Nobody wants to hire me, and Octo-Cat wants out anyway. Then there was that whole thing with Blaire yesterday."

"I still can't believe that girl would throw everything you've done for her back into your face." My grandmother's face turned red; her voice shook with rage.

"She was just trying to help—mostly herself—but hey."

"Awful, awful," Nan tutted while returning her attention to the groceries.

"It was pretty stressful yesterday, but at least it was something to do. I've been feeling adrift lately."

"The post-matrimonial blues?" she suggested. "That's not as uncommon as you might think. Your life is changing a lot right now. It's natural to feel off-balance."

"I love Charles. No regrets there. But he is so busy at work each day, and I have very little to do here. Plus the cats all keep to themselves and with you and Paisley gone, I just..." I shrugged. "Well, that's why I thought going back to school might be a good idea."

Nan nodded as she lined up the various jars of spices in a straight row. "I understand now. Do you have an idea of what you might like to study?"

The corners of my mouth turned down. "Honestly, I'm not sure. I love solving mysteries. I wish I could keep doing that."

"You could do it on the side if you have to. Maybe you'd enjoy being a policewoman?"

"Maybe," I said, even though I could never picture myself carrying a weapon on the regular. I'd been threatened one too many times to ever feel comfortable with that kind of power on my person.

Nan placed a hand on my upper arm and waited for me to meet her eyes before speaking. "You've been the Pet Whisperer for nearly three years now. You never stuck with anything else that long. It seemed this career was truly it. You're something special."

I sighed heavily. She was right. She was so right, but it was also no longer enough. "All good things must come to an end."

"Pish-posh. That's just what unhappy people say."

"Yeah, *me*. I mean, I'm mostly happy with my life. I just need more. Does that make sense?"

Nan placed a quick kiss on my cheek. "You've always been too big for this world, Angie. It's the thing I love most about you. I also have no doubt you'll find what you're missing—and soon. But right now, let's bake some scones. Could you preheat the oven for me?"

I loved Nan, but I also didn't think she understood the crux of my problem. She'd lived an adventure-filled life for twice as long as I'd led my comparatively mundane one. Nan had always been my best friend, my closest confidant, but this particular problem just didn't seem to be connecting. She and her husband were both retired and got to spend all day doing wonderful things together.

She also hadn't understood my anxiety over the whole Charm situation the day before, which made me wonder if our bond might be fraying a little bit.

We still saw each other most days, but not living together really limited our contact. And I was no longer the most important person in her world—her new husband Grant had stolen the spotlight from me.

Maybe I was finally growing up, standing on my own two shaky legs.

With little else to keep me occupied for the rest of the afternoon, I decided to call and check up on Grandma Lyn. Now that the Charm situation had resolved itself, I wanted to get her insights on having been ridiculed for her secret—the same secret I now shared.

"And she threatened to expose you?" Grandma Lyn asked with a gasp once I'd finished relaying all the details.

"She said she wanted to make me famous. Isn't that so silly?"

"Well, Dr. Doolittle was a very popular movie. The original, not this new CGI nonsense with that Ironman fellow."

I smiled to myself as I pictured the look on her face. It had to be a doozy to match the disgust that laced her usually sweet voice.

"Do you think people would be more accepting nowadays?" I ventured while picking at the skin on my elbow.

Grandma Lyn thought about this for a moment. "The world has changed a lot in recent years, but I just don't know, Angie. I wish I did, but it's impossible to guess what might happen if others were to find out."

"So far everyone has been very accepting of it. Nobody ever spoke bad about it until Blaire. And even she wanted to monetize my ability, not ridicule it."

We both sat silent for a moment. What was I trying to convince my grandmother of? Was it something I'd already decided for myself? I hadn't gotten this far in my conversation with Nan, but try as she might she would never understand—not the way someone who shared my ability could.

"Do you ever have regrets about what happened back when Mom was a baby?" I asked gently. I'd been curious for ages, but had never gathered the courage to ask. Until now.

Grandma Lyn didn't hesitate with her answer. "All the time. It's tough not to wish the past was different, but at the same time, I'm very happy where we've all landed in the present. If your mother hadn't grown up, she never would have met your father. Never would have given the world its greatest treasure—you."

And I was crying again.

Great.

11

I was on my own that evening, thanks to Charles wining and dining an important corporate client. Luckily, I had lots of Nan's famous blueberry scones to fill my belly for dinner. We'd already discarded the batch I'd been responsible for making. Somehow I had forgotten to add the salt, which ruined the finished product much more than one might assume.

By now, the cats had finished their lessons for the day, which meant they all hung close to me—a small and demanding pride of mismatched house-cats.

We'd decided to snuggle up and watch *The Wizard of Oz* together, seeing as Charlene had never seen it, and we were just to the part where

Dorothy meets the cowardly lion when my phone buzzed with a notification. I grabbed the device from the nearby coffee table and gasped when I noted what it was attempting to tell me.

Octo-Cat noticed me tense up right away. "What?" he asked, high-stepping across the couch and climbing onto my lap to bat at the phone. "What is it?"

"It's a new mess—"

"Angela, pause the movie first!" he cried with such astounding vigor it made me leap in my seat. I grabbed the remote control and clicked the stop button then revealed, "It's a new message from Charm."

Octo-Cat scrunched up his nose as if smelling something foul in the air. "Your bully? But I thought we figured out who it was, and UpChuck got them to stop. What now?" Ever since we'd returned from the honeymoon, Octo-Cat had gotten in the habit of calling my husband by that horrible nickname again. He claimed it was so as not to confuse Charlene and Charles, but I knew he just liked giving me grief.

"Was it really that nice girl Blaire? The one who adopted my mama?" Charlene mewled sadly.

"Unfortunately, yes." I hated this. Charlene was

still far too young to have to deal with issues like this, to know how much bad there was out there.

"I have never met a human with so many problems," Jacques said, stretching forward to expose his hairless webbed feet.

"And our first owner was murdered," his sister added eerily.

"Yup, thanks for that." I avoided arguing with the Sphynx cats whenever possible. They could go on and on without reprieve, and I just didn't have the time or energy to meet them part way.

"Well, go on and read the message," Octo-Cat prompted, rubbing his face against my phone impatiently.

"Right, okay." I swiped to open the social media app and held my breath as I read the words silently to myself. As soon as I'd finished, I let out a long, happy sigh.

"Don't just keep it to yourself. We're all invested now," Jillianne groused, then dragged her tongue across the wrinkles near her armpit. Those two were always pretending to groom themselves, but really I thought their feeble attempts just made them filthier than they were to begin with. It was why they got baths twice weekly, a chore that thankfully Charles took care of himself.

I turned the phone so Octo-Cat could read the new message from Charm and paraphrased for the others. "She says she's sorry and just wanted to double-check to make sure I'm not going to sue her."

"We *should* sue her," Octo-Cat said, greed lighting his amber eyes. "We could use the money to buy stock in Little Dog Diner."

"You're not playing the stock market," I warned immediately. "No freaking way."

Octo-Cat flattened his ears against his head. "Well, could we at least get some lobster rolls then?"

I rolled my eyes at him. "We literally just had them yesterday."

"Hey, the stomach wants what the stomach wants."

"I don't think that's how the expression goes," I corrected with a scowl.

"Can we please get back to the movie now?" Jacques snarled, then gingerly licked his fleshy thigh and added, "It's my favorite part."

"We will." I chewed on my lower lip as I worked through the flurry of thoughts that had just blanketed my brain. "First, can we talk about something real quick?"

Charlene jumped onto the back of the couch and crawled over to sit near my shoulder. Octo-Cat settled himself on my lap. The Sphynxes looked irritated, but offered no verbal argument, at least.

"This whole thing with Charm... Blaire... Well, it's got me thinking." I paused here, just in case any of the cats planned on complaining, offering commentary, or insulting my usual lack of foresight.

They remained blissfully quiet, and so I continued with my heartfelt plea for advice. "I became absolutely terrified when I thought some mystery stranger on the Internet would expose my secret. She seems to have backed off now, but what if it happens again with someone else? I got so keyed up when she messaged again today—so afraid. But what if I could avoid all that in the future? What if—?"

"You want to tell the world your secret," Octo-Cat interrupted, still poised on my lap. "As long as my life doesn't change in any way, I am all for it."

"I like that you can talk to us," Charlene offered in that cute squeaky voice of hers.

"We don't care what you do," Jillianne spoke up as a representative for both naked cats. "Just leave us out of it, and don't let any harm come to *our* human as a result."

The Sphynxes and I would probably always have a lukewarm relationship, but the same could be said of Octo-Cat with Charles—or as my cat preferred, UpChuck. Charlene was different since we had adopted her together, but our other pets were definitely one-human animals. Such was their nature; I couldn't fault them for that.

"Do you think I should come out on my own? You know, control the narrative?" I studied each of their unblinking expressions, trying to glean any insight as to whether this was a crazy idea—or a brilliant one.

Jacques was the one who spoke up first. "Again, don't care as long as our stipulations are met. Now can you put the movie back on already?"

I sighed and pressed play on the remote, bringing the cowardly lion's song-and-dance routine onto the screen.

"Angela," Octo-Cat said, pawing at my lap. "May I please see you in the kitchen? *Alone.*"

Uh-oh. Now I was really going to get it. Somehow I'd upset him without even trying. I was too focused on my own problems. I was—

"I had to play it cool for the others. You know,

be a cool cat and all that," Octo-Cat whispered as soon as we both made it to the kitchen and he'd had the chance to hop up onto the counter. "But I think you should do whatever makes you happy. Lately you haven't been—happy, that is—and I don't like that at all. You're much better company when you're not in a constant state of worry."

I reached forward to stroke his head between his ears. "But what will people say when they find out?"

"The ones who matter will be there for you, just like they always have. Screw the haters."

I glared at him. "Did you figure out how to turn off the parental locks on your iPad again?"

"So what if I did? That's not the point. The point is people live very small and complicated lives compared to us cats. A cat doesn't keep secrets or worry what others might think. A cat just is, and he's all the better for it."

I bit my lip to avoid pointing out that he'd just faked indifference for Jacques and Jillianne's benefit and only shared his true feelings on the matter once he had me alone. What he was saying made a lot of sense. I'd been keeping my secret for nearly three years and it was not easy. How much different would my life be if I simply stopped caring? If my secret was out in the open for all to see? Then it would be up to them to decide how they felt about it. The burden would be completely removed from my shoulders. I could finally rest.

"Well...?" Octo-Cat prompted when I still hadn't met his heartfelt words with a response. "Are you going to do it?"

"Tell you what, I'll sleep on it." I smiled as I stroked Octavius's striped fur. "But thank you for what you said. It means a lot to know you always want what's best for me."

"You're my human, and I love you." He let out a rumbling purr before abruptly falling silent. "But your happiness shouldn't ever come at the expense of mine. As long as you understand that, we'll be good."

I let out a soft laugh at that. "You're good. We're good."

Now the question was *would I be?*

I guessed I'd decide in the morning.

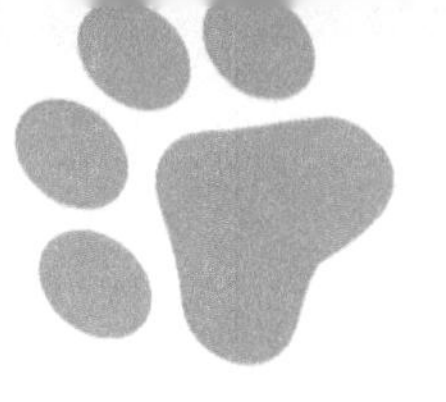

12

Well, I slept on it.

And by the next morning, I felt pretty confident about what I must do. For my own sake—really, for all of our sakes—I needed to come clean to the world about my strange ability.

I woke up early that day to spend a little time with Charles before he left for work, and he promised to support me in whatever was to come, reminding me once again that this was what our marriage vows were all about in the first place.

One by one, I called all the people who already knew, or at least the ones I'd confided in personally. Nan's Internet friends didn't need a heads-up on what was to come, but my family definitely did.

"How are you going to do it?" Mags asked when I called to tell her the news.

As much as this new plan had been dominating my mind lately, I still hadn't worked out all the details. That was another reason for calling those in the know—to get their advice. "I thought about writing out a speech, but I'd really rather speak from the heart."

"No, I mean, *how* are you going to do it?" Mags insisted, her pale eyes wide with intrigue. "Post a video on your page, call up that reality TV crew that filmed your wedding? Oh, I could interview you for my YouTube channel. Wax Nation already knows and loves you. I'm sure they'd be very supportive!"

I thought about this for a second. "I don't know," I admitted at last. "It feels really big coming out to your millions of subscribers, especially when they all follow you to see cool candle videos. I can't compete with that. And on the flip side, my own page only has, like, ten followers. Nobody will even see the video if I post there."

"So then the reality show guys?" my cousin suggested with an expression that told me exactly what she thought of that idea.

I shook my head adamantly. "No, they were unfair with Sharon. I wouldn't do that to her."

"Then what?" Mags wanted to know. Heck, I wanted to know too!

"I'll think on it some more and let you know when I figure things out," I promised.

"Okey dokey, smokey." A giant smile split Mags's face. "That's a new catchphrase I'm trying out. What do you think of it?"

I returned her smile, but no doubt had a mischievous glint in my eyes as well. "I'll keep thinking on my thing, and you keep thinking on yours."

"Ouch. Burn. Love you, Cuz."

"Love you. Bye."

After Mags, I called Grandma Lyn. I'd already decided for myself that I needed to come clean, but talking to all the people who loved me most in the world only made me more and more confident this would be the right next step for me in my life.

"I'm proud of you, Angie," Grandma Lyn cooed once she, too, had heard the news. "Being true to who you are while not being sure how the world will react is very brave. Just make me one promise."

"Sure, what?"

Grandma Lyn didn't use FaceTime, so I had no visual clues as to what was coming next. "Find someone you can talk to. Someone who's available now and will be there for you whatever happens next."

"But I already have so many people I can talk to," I argued gently. "You're one of them."

Grandma Lyn chuckled at this. "Yes, you'll always have me, but find a professional, too."

"Are you suggesting I'm crazy?" I teased, but I guess my playful tone didn't quite come across the phone line.

Grandma Lyn sighed. "I wish I would have started therapy earlier in life. It should be a requirement for every human, and it's extra required for you and your extraordinary life."

I promised her I would find someone to counsel me, then called Nan. It wasn't so long ago I would have told her before anyone else, but the added physical distance between us made everything so much harder these days.

Nan was, of course, incredibly supportive once I told her. I seriously didn't know why I ever doubted her.

"I think that's the right decision, dear, and if you think it is too, well, then there we go," she said with a warm grin.

"There we go," I repeated back. "Only I have no idea how I'm going to make my big reveal."

"Why, you'll do it on your parents' news show, of course."

Yes, of course!

My parents co-anchored a local news show, which was recorded and broadcast here in Blueberry Bay but served communities as far away as Massachusetts. It would be the perfect platform for what I needed to do.

I exhaled with relief. "Nan, you're a genius."

She clucked her tongue at this. "Well, yes, but we both already knew that, dear."

* * *

"And today we have a very special human interest story for our viewers," my dad announced, shuffling his papers on the news desk before him.

My mom sat at his side, her hair neatly curled and her lipstick perfect as she stared into the teleprompter with a charismatic grin. "That's right, Roman. We have a special guest in the studio, and it's none other than our daughter, Angie Longfellow."

I cleared my throat as the cameras panned toward me. Nan had wanted to dress me in some sparkly flapper-esque gown, but I'd insisted on wearing my favorite polka-dotted knee-length frock. Sure, it made me look a little like Minnie Mouse, but it also gave me the confidence to be myself, quirks and all.

"Hi, Mom. Dad," I replied with a huge practiced smile. That had been my parents' advice to me before we started the segment. *No matter what, just keep smiling.* So that's what I did now. I smiled so wide that my cheeks hurt. I even attempted to maintain my toothy grin while talking, which made my words come out somewhat muffled. "It's great to be here."

"Angie, tell us why you're here today," my dad enunciated far more clearly than I had, glancing quickly toward the teleprompter before he continued. "You have something you wanted to share with our viewers. Is that right?"

I nodded, swallowing down the freshly formed lump in my throat. I wanted to come clean with the world, but that didn't mean I wasn't incredibly nervous about finally voicing my secret aloud.

Apparently, I didn't respond fast enough because my mother spoke up next. "And you've brought somebody with you today, I understand."

That was the prompt I'd needed to shake myself free of the mental bonds that had immobilized me.

"Yes!" I practically shouted, forgetting about my smile for a moment as I reached under the news desk and grabbed a plastic pet carrier.

I set it on the desk and opened the metal door. Octo-Cat immediately strolled out.

"Well, hello there. You're very handsome," Mom cooed even though she'd seen Octo-Cat a million times before. "What's your name, big guy?"

"Octavius Maxwell Ricardo Edmund Frederick Fulton Russo Longfellow," my cat introduced himself with his usual pomp and flair.

I repeated the name for the viewers at home. "You can't understand him, but I do. My name is Angie Longfellow, and I can talk to animals."

A beat of silence passed before I added, "I suppose I should tell you how it all began. Almost three years ago, I was working at the law firm of Longfellow and Associates. Of course, back then it was called Fulton, Thompson, and Associates. And, well, there was this coffee maker..."

13

"How'd I do?" I asked eagerly once I'd finished my segment. Mom and Dad had to get back to the news, and Grandma Lyn said my exposure brought back too many painful memories for her to be physically in attendance but that she'd be cheering me on from afar. Charles, Grant, and Nan had both taken the full day off from their usual activities to support me, and they all gave me enthusiastic thumbs up as I rejoined them backstage.

"I was the main draw, of course," Octo-Cat crooned from within my arms, having refused to get back in his carrier once I'd gotten him out. "I mean, look at me. Who wouldn't want to talk to me?"

I laughed and shook my head, filling the others in on what my cat had just said.

In public.

With other people around.

I'd never been able to do that before, and it felt great to be able to do it now.

"Should we go home and have some pancakes?" Nan suggested after clapping her hands together to draw our focus. Not a single one of us could argue with that idea, and so the four of us headed back to the old manor house to celebrate.

And, well, I guess that was it.

I'd done it. I'd like to say that I felt different, better somehow. But honestly, I felt the same as always. Who knew how many people would even see my brief five minutes of fame? And out of those how many would actually believe it?

Some might assume I was a comedian. Others may think I was a fraud looking to make some money. Either way, they would now know the truth about what I could do, whether or not they chose to believe it.

"This will be wonderful publicity for your business," Nan said later when we were all seated with heaping stacks of flapjacks in front of us. You can add 'As seen on channel seven' to your website."

"I don't really have a website anymore," I admitted. I'd stopped running the recommended updates months ago and when I'd tried to log in a couple weeks ago, the entire site crashed.

Nan shrugged off my concern. "Then you can add it to your page."

"Do you really think people will want to hire me now?" I asked, my eyes wide with wonder.

"I can certainly give a great endorsement based on all the help you gave us at the Christmas Festival," Grant added as he sliced into his steaming stack of breakfast cakes.

"That's not a bad idea," Charles caught hold of this thread and pulled on it some more. "You should get testimonials from as many former clients as you can."

"One problem with that. Nobody was really an actual client, except the former mayor and I doubt he'd endorse me." Heat rose to my cheeks as all eyes zoomed toward me.

"They're still people you helped. I'm sure most of them would be more than happy to say a few nice words, dear," Nan threw her two cents into the pot as well.

"I haven't been thinking about any of that stuff, although I guess I should now that my big confession has been made." I popped a bite into my mouth and chewed before adding, "There's no going back now. It's out there."

"How do you feel?" Charles asked.

"The exact same," I admitted after swallowing that delicious mouthful of sugary, buttery mush.

Nan reached across the table for the syrup. "Well, nothing about you has changed, I suppose. I am very proud of you though, dear."

Charles scooted his chair so close to mine that our hips touched. "Me too, honey. I'm very proud of you."

"And I'm a proud step-grandfather," Grant said with a kindly chortle.

My phone buzzed in my pocket. "Oh," I cried, setting down my fork and knife to fish it out. "I have a new message on my page."

Grant's bushy eyebrows shot up. "Already? Well, that was fast."

"I'm not even one bit surprised," Nan stated triumphantly.

Seeing as the room was filled with my biggest supporters, I decided to read the message aloud. "Saw you on the news. You look really pretty..." My voice slowed as I continued to read, not liking where this was going one bit. "I would like to be your—" I stopped altogether here.

"Your what, Angie?" Charles prompted.

My cheeks burned with the flames of blazing embarrassment. "Your sugar daddy," I whispered, immediately pressing the button that would block the user.

"What's a sugar daddy?" Charlene asked from beneath the table.

"It's a man who makes delicious cookies for his family," Octo-Cat answered confidently. Lord help me.

My phone buzzed again. This time I read the message to myself before speaking up: *You're the Pet Whisperer, right? Can you get my dog to stop eating its own poop?*

Uh, that's not really what I do, I typed back. *Try the Dog Whisperer instead.*

"Everything okay?" Charles asked, trying to crane his neck to look at my phone, too.

I handed him the phone and sighed.

"Well, it's natural for a few crazies to come out of the woodwork with things like this," he offered, returning my device to me. "The point is you're getting attention now. Eventually the right people will find you."

* * *

Charles was typically right about almost everything, but this time he was very, very wrong.

As time passed, I received more and more inquiries that had nothing to do with my actual business or abilities. I also received a few messages with photo attachments that were—ahem—quite inappropriate and completely unwanted.

As much as I loathed it, I could handle people picking on me, but what I couldn't tolerate was how many chose to bother Charles at his work. A handful of strangers showed up each day, hoping to gawk or even score a bit of one-on-one time with the "magic coffee maker" that had gifted me with my powers.

Some even booked new client meetings just to get a closer look at where it all went down.

The net result was that Charles became even busier than he'd been before. He tried to keep a good face, but I could tell all the negative attention was bothering him.

And that was just the crazies.

Soon the bullies emerged, and—boy—did they let us have it. Charles went from being the most respected attorney in the entire region to the husband of that crazy woman who believed she could talk to animals.

Because the truth was, despite that heartfelt introduction on my parents' news show, very few people actually believed me about what I could do.

By the time a still shot of my televised interview turned into a meme, I was about ready to reach out to Blaire/Charm again and beg to take her up on her earlier offer of management. The only reason I didn't act on that urge was because it had become abundantly clear that there would be no money in this for anyone—least of all me.

Still, every day I dutifully scrolled through my messages, hoping beyond hope that there would be at least one authentic inquiry amongst the dozens of dreck.

Can you help me talk to my dead guinea pig? One woman asked. I had a number of stock replies to send to people now, and chose to send her the one that read, "Pet Whisperer P.I. doesn't offer the particular service you're looking for, but we wish you all the best!"

The next message in my inbox informed me that I was a danger to myself and society and that I belonged in a mental health institution. That was the fifth one this week. *Lovely.*

Farther down, a local rescue organization informed me that they would be happy to find Octavius a more stable household while I grappled with my own issues.

They honestly thought the most spoiled cat in the entire world needed to be rescued, or at least removed from my care.

And that was the final straw!

I couldn't take all this negativity anymore. Whatever I had expected from coming out with my ability it wasn't this.

In a fit of fury, I deleted my entire social media presence and slammed my laptop shut.

There, now nobody could make fun of me anymore. Why had I ever complained about being bored?

This was so, so much worse.

Once again, I'd failed—and this time it hurt more than ever.

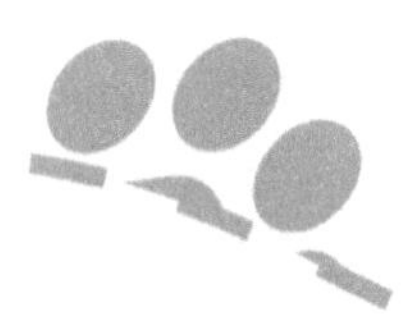

14

My head rested in Nan's lap as I cried my heart out.

"There, there," she said, slowly stroking my hair and making soft shushing noises.

I turned my patchy face to look up at her. "Why is this happening to me?" Nearly a week had passed since my big interview, and it had been less than two since I'd deleted my social media page and gone into hiding.

Charles had wanted to take a leave of absence to watch over me, but Nan had insisted she was up to the task. She brushed her hands across my cheeks to wipe away the tears. "The whole world's a stage, and they've only just realized you're a star," she offered sagely.

"I don't feel like a star." I sniffed. "I feel like a monster that's being hunted with pitchforks sharpened and torches lit."

"You aren't afraid to be different, to be yourself. A lot of people are threatened by that, I guess."

I sat up and swiped at my eyes. "That's where you're dead wrong. I'm afraid all the time."

"It will get easier," my grandmother assured me before slowly rising to her feet. "Let me go put on the kettle."

Normally, I'd follow Nan to the kitchen and stand with her while she prepared tea, but today I just didn't have the energy. Her little dog Paisley trotted after her to make sure she had company, but that left me alone.

The poor Chihuahua had tried so hard to lift my spirits, but my constant state of gloominess seemed to be wearing on her. Not that I could blame her. My emotions were cranked to the max, and every day they felt bigger, more unwieldy. Would I ever feel like myself again? I was seriously beginning to doubt it.

A knocking on the window behind me caught my attention, and when I turned I saw a familiar masked fur ball staring in at me.

I motioned for Pringle to move to the front door,

then grabbed a tissue from the end table en route to the entryway.

Pringle stood on his hind legs, holding onto his tail and brushing his fingers through it nervously. "I'm sorry to bother you at home," he said with his head dipped in reverence.

I offered him a momentary smile as I waved him inside. "You're not a bother. Come on in."

The trash panda shook his head. "No, I'm not allowed in the house."

"Unless you're invited. Remember our new rule?"

Pringle's eyes lifted cautiously to meet mine, and I gave an affirming nod. I just didn't have it in me to smile at the moment. The first one had taken it all out of me.

I watched with interest as the raccoon sucked in a deep breath and then slowly moved one foot over the threshold, still holding onto his ringed tail like some sort of security blanket. He let out the breath he'd been holding and slid his other foot past the doorway.

When he looked up at me with shining black eyes, I nodded again and motioned toward the living room. "Come on. Nan and I were just about to have some tea."

"What's that, dear?" Nan called from the kitchen, her voice extra chipper to balance my melancholy.

"Pringle's here!" I called back. "Can you grab some extra snacks so he can join us?"

Pringle's eyes grew wide, and he reached for his tail once again. "Really?"

"Really. Now hop up here and tell me what's going on." I patted the couch beside me.

This time Pringle only hesitated briefly before acting upon my invitation. "I came to check on you because I miss you. You didn't come out to read yesterday or the day before, and I just want to make sure you're doing okay."

My heart swelled in my chest. The very thing I was now being ridiculed over was also the same thing that had brought me so much joy, that brought me such kind and caring friends like Pringle.

"I'm sorry. We'll finish Merlin's adventure soon, okay?"

The raccoon shook his head and folded his hands in his lap. "That's not what I mean. You just never miss reading time. It made me worry."

"I'm okay, Pringle. Promise." I held his eyes, daring him to question me.

"Excuse me for saying so, but you don't look okay."

I laughed through a fresh wave of tears. "Remember how you like secrets so much? And watching people do crazy things on reality TV?"

He bobbed his head.

I don't know why I hadn't told Pringle all this before, especially when we still read together every day—or at least we had, until I officially shuttered Pet Whisperer P.I. and became too depressed to leave the house, even for the backyard. I guess I just enjoyed our little world of magical cats and a guaranteed victory for the good guys. It provided a nice escape from my current reality.

But now that the raccoon had come asking after me, I needed to tell him the truth. "Well, I went on TV and told everyone my secret, and let's just say there's been a poor response."

Pringle gasped. "Bad ratings?"

I nodded subtly. "Something like that."

"I'm sorry people didn't like your secret. Which one did you tell?"

"What do you mean which one did I tell? I only have the one secret."

"Did you tell people you can talk to animals, or did you tell them about the baby?"

"Excuse me, what?" I exploded, causing Pringle to jump back in fright.

"Pringle, I'm not—I don't..." I didn't know how to finish that. Was I getting fat? Is that why the raccoon thought the impossible?

Of course, Octo-Cat chose this precise moment to wake up from his nap and join us in the living room. "You're not what?" he asked suspiciously, whiskers twitching.

I could barely speak the word. Charles and I hadn't been trying for a baby, but we also hadn't *not* been trying. "Pregnant," I choked out hardly above a whisper.

My cat appeared almost bored. "Oh, that? No, yeah, you totally are."

"WHAT?!" I boomed. "You knew and you didn't tell me."

He yawned as if this conversation wasn't completely and unalterably life-changing. "I thought you were waiting to make it some big reveal. I didn't realize you hadn't figured it out yet."

"May I?" Pringle asked before reaching out to press one hand to my belly.

And now Nan returned with the tea and a tray of assorted snacks from the pantry. Paisley jumped up beside Nan and growled, the hair bristling on the little dog's back. Let's just say Pringle hadn't always been the nicest to her, and even if she'd forgiven him for his past sleights, she had a very hard time forgetting. Paisley hardly weighed more than five pounds; the poor thing needed to stay on high alert to stay safe.

"What did I miss?" Nan asked, staring pointedly at Pringle. I don't think she'd ever seen me willingly allow him in the house before, so the sight of him cozy on the couch took her rather by surprise.

"Nothing," I shouted, then pressed my lips in a firm line and muttered, "I mean, nothing out of the usual."

Thankfully, she let it go. I couldn't get her hopes up until I knew for sure.

It took everything in me to act normally while we drank our tea and munched on our snacks. Well, at least I wasn't crying over my spoiled reputation anymore. I had a new problem to worry about now—no, not problem—a new *change*, and this one felt even bigger than revealing my hidden ability and closing my business.

Was I ready to be a mother?

That would certainly keep me busy, but not for another nine months or so. And when the time came, would I be able to survive all the work that came with a newborn while Charles worked practically one-hundred hours per week? If I had one baby now, would I just keep on having babies until my whole life became mommyhood? That wasn't necessarily a bad thing, but it was different.

And also very, very scary.

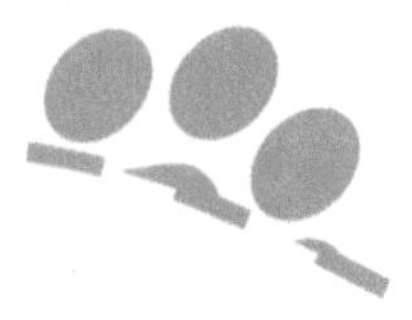

15

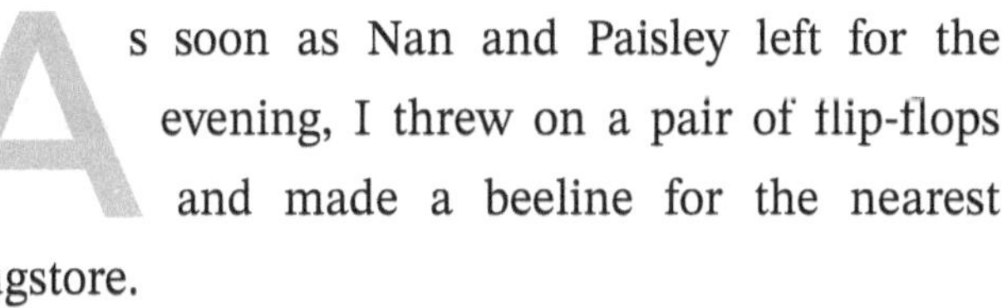

As soon as Nan and Paisley left for the evening, I threw on a pair of flip-flops and made a beeline for the nearest drugstore.

To buy a pregnancy test.

Me.

My heart had now taken up residency in my throat, threatening to cut off my air all together. Charles and I had decided to leave our family planning to fate, which hadn't seemed like that big of a deal when we'd originally discussed it. But now that I could be jobless and with child? I was nowhere near mastering my domestic lessons? In fact, I was but ready to give up on them altogether. And without a job, I couldn't justify hiring someone else to come in and run the household. That would make me entirely useless in my own disaster of a life.

I couldn't justify labeling myself a full-time stay-at-home cat mom, and even they had found plenty to keep themselves busy without me.

Where did that leave me?

And did I want this? Did I want it right now at this very point in my life?

One way or another I'd get on board, but it was hard not to feel completely overwhelmed as I plucked the pink and white box off the shelf and buried it in my basket beneath a healthy-sized layer of selections I'd made in the candy aisle.

This particular pharmacy didn't have a self-checkout lane, which meant I was at the mercy of the cashier. Hopefully, she wouldn't comment on the pregnancy test or ask any questions that I was not prepared to answer.

Just to be sure though, I pulled out my phone and pretended to take an important call. Sure, it was rude, but desperate times and all that.

Imagine my shock and embarrassment when the phone actually rang with an incoming call. Heat flooded my cheeks as I clicked to answer.

"Hello?" I muttered, avoiding eye contact with the cashier as I spoke.

"Angie," my husband sounded almost relieved as he shouted into the phone. "Can you be ready to go out in one hour? I'll swing home and pick you up for dinner. Wear something dressy. We're going to Fernando's."

My mouth salivated at this information. Fernando's was the swankiest restaurant in all of the Bay, one to which we almost never had cause to visit. Did Charles know I needed some extra TLC today? Whatever the case, it would provide the perfect setting to tell him about the baby—if there even was a baby.

I smiled as I handed the cashier my credit card. "I can be ready," I informed Charles.

"Sorry for the short notice," my husband continued. "I've had this thing planned for weeks. Only now he's insistent you come, too."

"Wait. It's not just us?" I felt like I was going to be sick.

"Oof, sorry. I thought you knew I had the thing with Richard Fulton tonight. He's up from Florida this week and asked if we could talk business. We set it up at the wedding reception actually. I put it on our shared calendar."

I took my card back from the cashier and grabbed my overstuffed shopping bag before hurrying back to the parking lot. "Sorry," I murmured. "I've just had a lot on my mind lately, and you've been so busy... But yeah, I'll be ready in an hour. See you soon. Love you."

* * *

I debated waiting until after tonight's dinner to take my test, but quickly decided that was stupid, that I absolutely could not wait to know the truth.

So I peed on a stick, and...

Yup, pregnant. With child. In the early days of motherhood.

Things were moving along quite briskly on the family front, even if they were dead in the water when it came to my career. It would be incredibly difficult to keep mum during tonight's dinner, but this also felt like the kind of news a wife should tell her husband in private.

I could share the news when we were getting ready for bed, right in front of our enormous bathroom mirror as we brushed our teeth side by side. Charles would be ecstatic. Of that, I had no doubt.

His enthusiasm would help build mine, and

everything would be fine, just fine. I wasn't unhappy, just shocked. Bringing another life into this world gave me a ticking clock when it came to figuring out my own.

I sat motionless on the edge of the tub for what felt like hours as I tried to make sense of it all. My phone buzzed with a text from Charles stating that he and Fulton were leaving the law firm now. That meant I had about fifteen minutes to give myself a pep talk while putting the finishing touches on my look.

"You've got this," I whispered to my reflection as I dragged a coral lipstick over my mouth. "You'll be a great mom. I mean, look at Octo-Cat, he had no idea we'd be bringing Charlene home, and yet he's such a devoted dad. You'll be that too. Devoted. Not a dad, but a mom. A darn good one."

"I'm glad I could inspire you, Angela," Octo-Cat said from the doorway. I hadn't even heard him approach. "And you aren't alone in this. I'd be happy to give you parenting lessons."

"I thought cat lessons were supposed to be for cats only."

"I can adapt portions to fit the human experience. Just say yes and be grateful. You don't turn down Mozart when he's offering piano lessons."

I blinked hard at this assertion, although the analogy shouldn't have surprised me one bit. Octo-Cat had always thought highly of himself in the way all cats did. Now if I could just bottle that confidence for myself.

"I'd love some lessons," I answered as I breezed past him and headed downstairs. Charles would be here any minute, and I was ready.

I was so not ready.

I'd never been good at keeping secrets, but now I had to sit through the next two hours making small talk and pretending my entire life hadn't just changed in an instant.

Charles held my hand under the table and gave me the occasional reassuring squeeze. He could tell I was upset, but he thought it was about the other thing—about how I'd become a local laughingstock. Well, I was still rather unhappy about that, but it was no longer the star of my inner anxiety show. I'd just risked an awful lot to rid myself of one secret, and already I had a brand-new one clawing at my conscience.

It didn't help that I noted the curious eyes of the

staff and other diners landing on me again and again; each time, muted whispers followed. They were talking about me, calling me crazy or a fraud. One person even brought me a print-out of the meme they'd made from my interview and asked me to autograph it. *Fabulous.*

"Is it true?" Fulton asked over the salad course. "Can you really...?" He dropped his voice and leaned in conspiratorially. "Talk to animals?"

I twisted the cloth napkin that lay on my lap and nodded meekly.

Fulton took a sip from his water goblet and asked, "Is that why you were so eager to adopt Aunt Ethel's cat, because you'd befriended him?"

I nodded again. "It's how I knew your aunt had been murdered in the first place. Octo-Cat told me." It was easier to just agree than to explain the long and tortuous road Octo-Cat and I took to truly become friends. Earning a cat's trust took work and lots of it.

Fulton leaned back in his chair. "Well, I'll be. I feel silly for not having noticed all that time, but how could I? It's not a very common thing now, is it?"

I glanced up at Fulton to find him watching me.

"So you believe me?" I asked, then held my breath as I waited for his answer.

"Of course I believe you, Angie. I've always known you to be focused, kind, and smart as a whip. Why on earth would you lie about something like this?"

I let out a strangled laugh of relief. At least there was one person who didn't seem to think of me differently after finding out what I could do. Maybe it was a good thing I'd come tonight, after all.

"Now that we've settled in, allow me to tell you why I wanted to speak with you both tonight." Fulton traded his water goblet for a wine flute and raised it toward my husband. "Charles, you're the most brilliant young attorney I've ever had the privilege to work with, and I'd like to offer you a job. How would fewer hours with more pay suit you?"

Charles tensed beside me, but it didn't seem like Fulton noticed. "That sounds fantastic."

The other lawyer bobbed his head enthusiastically. "I thought you might say that. I've been asked to come on as a partner at my friend's very successful firm, and I agreed, provided I could nominate a junior partner to come with me. It's a slight demotion according to the official job title, but everything about it is bigger and better. They stick to the forty hour work-week there. No more drowning in overtime. You'll have time for a home life too. Imagine that."

I didn't know what Charles was thinking in that moment, but I was already imagining this new life just as Fulton had urged. I didn't care about the money, not really. We'd always had enough, thanks to my husband's brilliance and my cat's trust fund. But to have that time together? It would be a dream come true, especially with a baby on the way. I knew Charles was proud of the progress he'd made with his firm, but I hoped it wasn't so much that he would refuse to leave when given a better opportunity. I would definitely encourage him to take it, provided he didn't come to that conclusion on his own.

Everything was perfect, until the corners of Fulton's mouth turned down as he revealed, "There's just one catch. The job is out of state, and would require you to relocate."

16

"I'm not going to take the job," Charles told me once we'd dropped Fulton off at his hotel and had begun our drive home. "Your whole life is here. Your family. I can't ask you to give that up."

The fact that this new dream opportunity was in a completely different state sullied the offer a great deal. Fulton hadn't even told us which state it would be in, instead claiming that we shouldn't spoil our time together going over the finer details —not until Charles knew whether or not he'd even be willing to consider relocation. Fulton needed to know whether we were open to the general idea, and then he would put an official package together to offer my husband.

And already Charles was dead-set against the

whole thing. I still didn't know exactly how I felt, but I did think it was worth proper consideration, especially once I gave Charles one very important piece of the puzzle that until now he'd been missing.

"It's true that if we move, I'll miss Nan and Grant, and Mom and Dad, and of course, Paisley," I admitted softly. "But right now I spend all day missing you. And working all those long hours can't be good for your health."

He shook his head, keeping his eyes on the road as he drove. "I'll bring on an additional partner. Share the load more."

"Which directly impacts your salary, and without me working right now, that could be a real problem," I pointed out. But these were all very generalized arguments, things Charles probably already knew. I needed to tell him what he didn't know, and unfortunately I'd need to do it before we got back home for the night.

"Look, Fulton's a great guy. I really like him, I do. But your happiness comes first, Angie. He reached across the car to grab my hand and hold it in his. "Always and forever."

"My happiness comes second," I whispered,

seeing my opportunity and grabbing it with both hands.

"What do you mean? Of course I put you above me. I—"

"I'm pregnant," I chose that precise moment to reveal. "So I would think our baby comes first."

Charles accidentally tapped the brake causing the car behind us to honk an angry warning. My husband said nothing as he maneuvered into a strip mall parking lot and cut the engine.

"Charles? Is everything okay?" I asked, leaning forward to try to see his face.

He'd put both hands onto the top of the steering wheel and rested his forehead on top of them, his shoulders moved up and down but no sound escaped him.

"Charles?" I prompted again. This was not the reaction I'd expected. Was he upset? Overwhelmed? Frankly, I couldn't tell.

Finally Charles lifted his head, his entire face was red with emotion. "Angie," he whispered, his voice cracking. "Honey, I love you so much. And this is the best news ever."

He leaned forward to capture me in a kiss.

"I'll take this job if that's what you want," he said after we'd parted. "Or I'll take another job. I'll quit working altogether, and we can rent an RV and live off the land." He took a moment to laugh at his own ineptitude before continuing, "Okay, so I don't know what I'm talking about, but I do know that I love you so much. And somehow already I love our baby so much. I'll do anything, whatever it takes, to make sure the two of you have the best life."

"You'll be such a great dad." I reached out to stroke his hair, tucking an errant strand behind his ear. He'd been too busy with work to get a haircut, but I liked the shaggy look on him. "Let's ask Fulton to put that package together so we have all the information, and then we'll take a couple days to talk it over, think about what would be best for our family's future. The right decision will come to us. I have no doubt."

* * *

When we'd pulled off into the strip mall to talk things out, Charles had inadvertently ended up parking near my go-to pet supply store, Frank n' Beans. And since we were already there, I asked if he wouldn't mind me running in to pick up a few supplies for the cats.

Truthfully, I was still annoyed with Octo-Cat for

knowing about my pregnancy and choosing not to share that little tidbit with me. Then again, animals did things differently—and cats, most of all. I suspected that in some warped way, he thought he was doing me a favor. Ha!

So now tonight we would tell the others, provided they didn't already know, and have an intimate celebration—just me, Charles, and our four favorite felines.

While Octo-Cat preferred his treats in the form of grilled shrimp and lobster rolls, the Sphynx cats loved creamed salmon, especially when they could lick it directly from a little tube rather than having me plop it onto a cold plate. And because I wouldn't have time to get out to Misty Harbor before the diner closed, I settled on an assortment of new treats, filling my basket to the brim with various kitty delicacies. It would be fun to try them all out and see who liked what.

"Please bring your final purchases to the register. We're just about to close," Frank called from the front of the store. I hadn't seen him when I entered. He must have been in the back, taking care of stock. Sometimes he moved around this place like a ninja.

I smiled as I approached the checkout counter.

"Hi, Frank," I said as I plopped my basket down between us.

"Oh, Angie, hi." He immediately began scanning my items, glancing at me as we chatted. "It's been a long time. I was hoping you'd stop in again soon."

"Sorry, it's been hectic," I mumbled. I liked Frank, but I was also eager to get back to Charles and eager to share our big news with the rest of our household, which meant my tolerance for idle chit-chat was at a minimum.

"Yeah, I saw your interview. Really cool." Frank fumbled a bag of treats, then looked up at me askance. "Is it all true? You know, what you can do?"

I nodded and averted my eyes. "Yeah, unfor-tunately."

"Why is it unfortunate? If I could have any superpower, that's exactly the one I would want to have."

"It's not really a superpower," I hedged, even though I'd thought of my ability in that exact way too many times to count.

"It is to me," Frank enthused as he finished ringing up my massive quality of cat treats. He paused again. Even the massive Darth Vader helmet on his T-shirt seemed to wait with bated breath. "Um, I hope it's not asking too much, but I was wondering if maybe you could do me a favor? Or if you'd rather, I could pay you? I'm just in a pretty desperate spot with Beans. He's not eating, and he's been avoiding me, too. I'm really worried about him."

"That sounds like something you want to address with your vet," I answered briskly, hoping I wasn't coming across as too cold.

"I did, and there's nothing physically wrong with him. If I could just understand what's going on in that fluffy little head of his—" Frank stopped abruptly and sighed. "I'm bothering you, I'm sorry. I wouldn't ask if it weren't of vital importance."

My hand drifted to my elbow to pick and twist at the skin, a nasty nervous habit. "It's just... I don't do that anymore," I tried to explain, soft yet firm. "I closed my business a couple days ago."

Frank's face crumpled in on itself. He seemed just seconds away from flooding the place with a hot wave of tears.

"But I can help you with Beans," I decided aloud. And really what choice did I have? Frank wasn't mocking me like the others. He truly needed my help, and I'd be a horrible friend if I said no. "Is Beans here now?"

Frank lit up, taking on an energy I hadn't seen from him before. "He's somewhere around here. Maybe he'll come out if he knows you're here to help."

I glanced toward the glass door before he could hurry off in search of his feline co-clerk. "Would you mind locking that to give us some privacy? I'm still kind of shy when it comes to showing off my ability, especially given the response I've received since going on the news."

Frank dutifully rushed over to twist the lock and then turned back to me with the biggest smile I'd ever seen in all my life. "Tell you what, if you can help, your order is on the house."

I gasped at his offer. "But, Frank, that's like two-hundred dollars' worth of cat treats."

But he just shook his head, continuing to smile like a man who'd just had every last one of his dreams come true. "You're about to save my cat's life," he insisted. "The least I can do is spoil yours a little."

17

t took all of five minutes to discover that Beans had been avoiding his owner as a means of protest. Frank was a proud and vocal vegan. While he didn't exactly like his cat's biological need for meat, he understood it enough to allow him a seafood-only diet.

Except Beans absolutely hated it.

The first time I'd met the cat he'd bribed me into bringing him a raw steak in exchange for the information I needed to solve a mystery, one that landed particularly close to home.

Beans had then managed to sneak some more red meat a few weeks later at my wedding. Subsequently, he hadn't been able to stomach his "fish food" since and decided to mount a silent protest.

Upon learning this, Frank marched straight to the premium wet food and grabbed a can of the juiciest beefiest pate, which Beans tore into with gusto, singing both our praises. My work there done, I insisted on paying for my wealth of treats, but Frank insisted even harder that it would be on the house.

Back at home, Charles helped me open up every single container of treats and sprinkle a few from each onto the kitchen floor for our eager team of taste testers.

"Tonight we're celebrating the new addition to our family," I announced once the cats had all gathered around.

"It's about time you celebrated Charlene," Jillianne chirped before lowering her face to inhale some salmon-flavored soft treats.

"No, not Charlene." I moved my hand to my abdomen. Was there really a baby in here? Gosh, that would take some time to get used to. "Charles's and my baby."

"I thought *I* was your baby," the kitten whined, her jaw dropping open and partially chewed treats spilling out onto the floor.

"Our human baby," I corrected with a serene smile. "But we can absolutely throw Charlene a party too!"

"It's okay," the kitten said with a shrug that suggested it might not be. "Besides we already knew about your baby, but Papa Octo-Cat told us not to say anything," she said before grabbing a cat nip crunchy and munching away happily.

Jacques turned his nose up at the assortment of goodies offered. I would have to break out a tube of creamed salmon for him, but only after we finished our conversation. "I, for one, don't see why we're celebrating now. Shouldn't we wait for you to birth the litter first?"

"Not a litter! Just one!" I shouted before the true horror of that scenario could seep in. "Believe me, one will be more than enough."

"I don't like these treats," Octo-Cat stated flatly. "Can I have a lobster roll?" He paused for a moment then added a snide, "Please."

But before I could respond, my phone rang in my purse. I grabbed it and headed to the other room for a bit of privacy—or to get a short break from the cats, take your pick.

"Christine? What's up?" I asked, when I saw who was calling. It was Grizabella's owner, which made the two of us in-laws, even though she didn't know it yet.

"Is it true?" the other woman asked pointedly instead of offering a greeting. "You can talk to animals?"

Oh, that again. Every time I tried to move on to something else, the chaotic mess that came from sharing my secret dragged me right back in.

"I'm sorry I didn't tell you sooner, Christine. I mean, it all happened really fast, and—"

"How long have you been able? Since before we met?"

"Yes," I admitted. "Again I'm really so—"

Christine interrupted me with a spirited chuckle that instantly put me at ease. "I'm not mad. In fact, I think a small part of me always suspected. But I always told myself you were simply a devoted pet owner. I'm glad I'm not crazy."

"Nope, you're not crazy, though I sometimes think that I am." I paused for a moment before dropping the confetti bomb. "Did you know our cats are married?"

Christine let out another sharp laugh, and here I had worried she was mad at me when this call started. "Ha, I guess that makes us family!"

"Wait, how did you find out? Was it that horrible meme?" My stomach churned as I called up the unflattering image of myself that had taken the local Internet by storm.

My friend quickly put me at ease—or made things a whole lot worse. "Meme, no. There was an article about it on Buzzfeed. I called as soon as I saw it."

Buzzfeed? Great. That meant I was now getting national—possibly even international—attention. "I guess my secret's really out now."

And here I thought that the possibility of moving somewhere new would free me from the ridicule I'd received locally. Apparently not.

"The article was mostly click bait, to be honest," Christine was quick to explain. "There were a couple sentences about you and then the rest of it was a listicle about the top ten questions the staff wished they could ask their cats."

I let out a slow breath. "Anything good?"

"I'll send you the link," she promised.

An awkward pause followed, which led me to ask, "So you really don't care that I can talk to animals? Or that you had to find out the way you did?"

"Angie, I know things are different in your small town where everyone knows everybody. But it's different in the city. There's way too many people to keep track of here, let alone in the whole rest of the world."

"But people don't believe me." That was the one thing I couldn't get past. I was used to people thinking I was silly, but not a liar. And definitely not an unfit cat mother.

"So what if they don't believe you," Christine practically shouted. "At worst, you're a charismatic airhead, right? People will forget about it as soon as the next Florida Man article hits the news circuit. Maine Woman thinks she can talk to animals, cute. Florida Man wrestles alligator on a dare and loses big, now that's crazy."

I chuckled at this, wondering what it might be like to talk to an alligator, what kind of stories he might have to tell. "You definitely have a way of putting things into perspective. How are you? How are Grizz and the others?"

"We're doing just great, but it's not me I'm worried about." Christine's voice softened. "How are you handling the fallout?"

"It's been rough," I confessed and bit my lip.

"Maybe it's time you come for another visit. We'd love to have you!" It was true that Nan, Octo-Cat, Paisley, and I had enjoyed our last road trip out to see her and Grizabella, and I definitely wanted to bring Charles along for a future visit, but we simply had too much going on at present. And as much as I'd love to confide in Christine, I knew better than to share the news of the baby during the first trimester, and even more than that, I knew better than to tell her about our possible move within earshot of the cats.

"We'd love to have you have us," I said instead. "I've just got a lot going on at the moment, but I'll call you back soon, okay?"

"You better!" Christine chirped before offering a quick goodbye.

"Everything okay?" Charles asked as I padded back into the kitchen. Octo-Cat and Jacques had already dispersed due to their apparent dissatisfaction with the treats on offer, but our two female cats happily picked up the snacking slack.

"Yeah, that was just Christine. She saw an article online and wanted to check in with me," I explained.

"Word is really spreading, huh? Are you okay?"

"I will be," I said as my husband wrapped his arms around me.

Octo-Cat ran back in the kitchen so quickly, he had a hard time stopping himself from skidding across the linoleum floor. "Did you say Christine? How is my beautiful Grizz?"

"She's doing great," I answered without hesitation. I knew better than to suggest anything else or to confess that Christine and I hadn't even discussed her.

Octo-Cat swooned, dramatically flopping onto his side. "Ah, my lovely bride. Sweet, sweet Grizz. Our daughter looks more and more like her every day."

Charlene was a stray black kitten and Grizzabella was a pedigreed Himalayan, but okay. Whatever made him happy.

"Congrats on the baby, by the way. I'm glad Charles wasn't neutered like I was."

I practically choked on my own saliva, such was my surprise at that statement.

"Angie, are you okay?" Charles tapped me on the back until I stopped coughing. "What's he saying?"

"Let's just go to bed. It's been a long day!" I said before running toward the stairs, praying there wouldn't be any more awkward questions.

Such was life with cats. Never a dull moment!

18

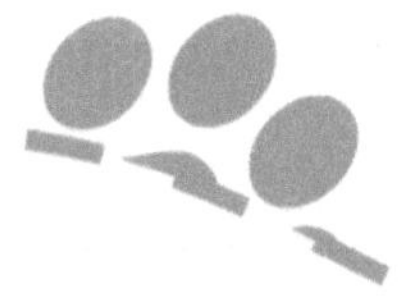

t took two full days to receive the official job offer from Fulton, and when my husband shared it with me, my eyes practically bulged out of my head. "You've got to be kidding me!"

Charles laughed. "I know he said more pay, but I've got to admit, that number is way higher than I was expecting."

"Not the salary, the location," I insisted pointing at that detail on the computer screen. "It's a sign. Don't you think?"

I grabbed both of his hands in mine, this newfound certainty filling me with blissful release. "Charles, you have to take it."

Apparently, my husband didn't have the same

confidence I felt. "What about Nan? And your parents? Your life here?"

"Well, that's why they make air travel and video calls." I flashed him a goofy smile, but he still appeared worried. I needed to take a different approach.

I moved behind him to rub at his shoulders, keeping my voice soft and even. "Just because we move away doesn't mean we have to be out of touch. Besides, this offer is incredible, especially as we start our family."

Charles turned to nuzzle my cheek, letting his warm breath fan over my skin. "Are you sure?"

"If you don't accept it, then I will," I half-joked. "Do you think Fulton will care that I don't have a law degree?"

Finally Charles's mood lightened, and he let out a laugh. "If there's one thing I learned early on about you, my sweet Angie, it's that you can make anything work if you want it bad enough."

He gave me a quick kiss before getting up to call and accept Fulton's offer, leaving me to my thoughts for a moment. I replayed my husband's words as I settled myself on the couch.

I could make anything work if I wanted it bad enough. What did that mean when it came to my

P.I. business? Had I simply not wanted it? Or had it lost all appeal when Octo-Cat chose to retire to focus on his new feline family? Had some small part of me already sensed the new life growing within me?

I couldn't answer any of those questions with any real certainty. But I'd started to suspect that maybe I had to break my life a little in order to rebuild it. I needed to bring old adventures to an end in order to be ready for all the amazing ones that came next.

I may have given up my title as Pet Whisperer, P.I., but I'd taken on the equally compelling new ones of wife and mother. Something good was coming to an end so that I could have something even better—something absolutely fantastic.

Charles returned and lowered himself gently onto the couch beside me. Our baby was hardly the size of a poppyseed, but he'd been extra careful around me since learning about that tiny seed.

"He's giving me a month to wrap things up here and even offered to help with the sale of the house. He said he had lots of interest after his aunt died, but when he found out you wanted it, he put them all off."

"That's really nice of him." I didn't think

Richard Fulton realized how much he'd impacted my life for the better. He'd paved the way to my meeting both Octo-Cat and Charles, inarguably the two most important men in my life. Speaking of Octo-Cat... "I guess that just leaves one thing."

"Telling everybody," Charles agreed. "How do you think Nan will take it?"

"She'll understand. I'm not afraid about that. I do worry about Jacques and Jillianne, though. They've been uprooted so many times in the last few years, and now we're moving them again."

"What about us?" The Sphynx cats hissed in terrifying unison as they sauntered into the living room to join us.

"Well, speak of the devils," Charles said with a laugh.

"We might as well tell them all now," I decided, more than ready to get it over with. I had a pretty good idea of how Octavius might respond, but he often found new and irritating ways to surprise me. "Octo-Cat! Charlene!"

"Tell us what?" Jillianne rasped as she claimed a spot on Charles's lap.

"I'm coming! Hold your ponies!" Octo-Cat yowled from somewhere upstairs. I decided not to tell him how badly he'd butchered the expression, and instead waited patiently until we were all together.

Charles and I sat side by side, our hands laced together, as we presented a united front as heads of the family.

"Guys," I said slowly, unsure of the best words for conveying this life-changing news. "Something really important happened today. Charles accepted a new job."

Octo-Cat yawned. "How quickly you forget, Angela. We don't care as long as it doesn't affect us." *Oh, boy.*

"That's the thing." I worked hard to keep the nervousness out of my voice. This was big news, but good. Surely they'd see that once I had the chance to explain everything, right? I cleared my throat before continuing. "It does affect you this time. Very much so, in fact."

Charlene flattened her ears against her tiny head. "What's happening? I'm scared."

"No need to be scared. It's a good thing, I promise. It will just take a little adjusting for all of us."

Charles squeezed my hand. "What are they saying? Is there anything I can do to help?"

I squeezed back. "It'll all be okay. I've got this."

Octo-Cat's tail began to swish wildly behind him. "I don't like the sound of this."

Time to rip off the Band-aid. "The new job is pretty far away. We'll have to sell this house and move into a new one."

"Absolutely not!" Octo-Cat bellowed, poofing up like a cat on Halloween. "I refuse to leave this house. You know how special it is to me. It's where my former owner lived and died, and if you force me to leave, I will—"

I raised one hand to silence him, surprised when it actually worked. "Octo-Cat, you don't understand. The new job is in Boulder, Colorado. You know, with Grizabella."

The tabby's mouth dropped open, and all four cats stared up at me with wide eyes.

"I don't like it here," Jillianne said from atop my husband's lap. "Too drafty." She shook to emphasize her point.

"Yeah, we don't care where we live as long as we have each other—and Charles, of course," Jacques clarified as he resettled himself on the chair.

"And Charlene! We also need Charlene!" Jillianne quickly added.

"Will we really get to live with Mama Grizz?"

The small black kitty cried, eyes shining with the potential promise of happiness.

"Not *with*, but *near*. We'll be able to spend lots of time together once we're settled in."

Octo-Cat still hadn't spoken since my latest reveal.

I lowered my face so that I was at his level and asked, "Well, what do you say?"

He closed his mouth, then opened it again like a fish gaping for water. When finally he spoke, it was to complain. "You nearly gave me a heart attack, Angela. You really need to work on your delivery. If you would have just rearranged the facts in a more pleasing order, I would not have had such a cloying response."

My chest unclenched as I let out an enormous sigh of relief. "I'm sorry for that," I said, reaching out to stroke his head.

Octo-Cat shook off my attempts to pet him, rose to all fours, and peered up at me with obvious agitation. "Well?" he shouted.

"Well *what?*" I asked, more than a little confused.

"How soon can we leave?" And with that he took off running toward the stairs. "I'm going to start packing!"

Looked like we were all on board.

Yes, including baby.

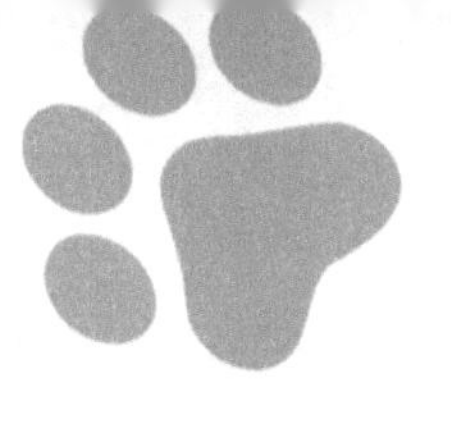

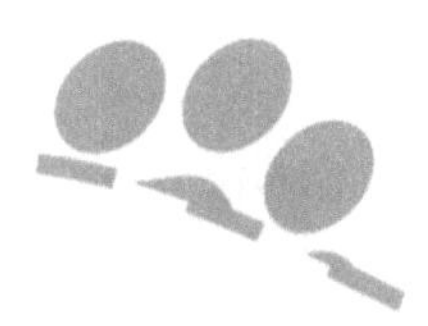 

19

I'd expected a bit more protest, but everyone was truly happy for Charles and me about this new chapter in our lives, especially once I revealed my pregnancy.

"You better have a room for me, because I am going to visit all the time!" Nan declared the moment she found out. "I'm going to be a Great-Nan!"

"You're already the greatest," I said, saddling her with a huge hug.

Paisley was a bit harder to convince. "But you're my Mommy, and I'll miss you," she whimpered.

I picked her up and held her like a baby, gently rubbing her tummy as we talked. "I'll miss you too. In fact, I've already been missing you since you and

Nan moved out. But you know Nan is your real Mommy, right? She's the one who rescued you from the shelter and has given you such a good life since."

The tri-color Chihuahua wagged her tail furiously. "I know. I guess I just always thought of myself as having two mommies."

"That's sweet, Paisley, and that doesn't have to change. No matter how much distance we put between us, our hearts will always be connected." I bent down and placed a small kiss between her huge triangle ears.

"And you'll come back to visit?"

"Lots and lots. I'll be back so often, you'll get sick of me," I promised, giving her a kiss on her pink tummy. And that's all it took for her to go back to being her usual spunky self, thank goodness.

* * *

The hardest person to tell, of course, was Grandma Lyn. We'd only just been reunited after decades of searching on her part, and now I was voluntarily moving away.

"Are you upset?" I asked her after I'd made my big announcement.

"No, of course not. As your grandmother, I want what's best for you, and you seem really excited."

"I am excited, but I'm going to really miss having you nearby."

Grandma Lyn cleared her throat and placed each of her palms flat on the table. "Actually, if it's okay with you, I think I'd like to come, too. I can get my own place, but I'd just like to be nearby."

"What about Mom? She'll still be here," I argued, even though I loved the thought of bringing her with us for our fresh start.

My grandmother looked me straight in the eye as she explained, "Your mother already lived so much of her life before I ever found her. You have too. I can't miss watching your little one grow up. It's like I'm being given a fresh chance, as if the universe is finally intent on setting things right."

"I like that. And I'd love for you to come with us."

* * *

As the days wore on, I found myself revisiting all my old haunts—small businesses I'd supported, restaurants I'd frequented, crime scenes I'd stumbled upon. My whole life had been lived out here in this place, and even though I knew I'd be back for frequent visits, I still felt like I needed to say goodbye to the places just as much as the people. As I ventured around the Bay, I attracted some pointed stares and curious whispers, but I also sensed that my little televised interview was starting to become yesterday's news. Christine had been absolutely right about that. Now I was just Maine Woman, and soon I'd be out of people's minds altogether.

For years I'd focused on hiding my ability to talk with animals. Hiding that secret had become just as big a part of my identity as the secret itself. Then I'd decided to come clean and the community's collective response had defined my existence for a brief time after that.

And now?

Now neither of those things determined how I lived my life. I did that. The people and animals I held dear helped, too.

When I first learned I could talk to animals, I had thought of myself as a freak, then I'd redirected all that energy into becoming some super-powered sleuth. Now I realized that, more than anything, the main thing my ability had brought me was more friendships, more love. A richer and fuller life.

I'd been able to help animals who might otherwise not have found any. And I didn't need an official title to keep on doing that. Even if I was no longer a private investigator, I could still put good in the world, still help bridge communication between human and animalkind, and—yes—even solve the occasional mystery that came my way.

I made my ability. It didn't make me.

It wasn't sharing my secret, but rather realizing that last bit which truly freed me.

Similarly, I realized it wasn't bricks and drywall that made a home, but the people who occupied it. I loved our old manor house, but not in the same way Octo-Cat always had. Other than the time he spent with his mother as a kitten and those few short months when I'd forced him to live in my former rental with me, this manor had always been his place of residence. It was where he'd met and fallen in love with Ethel Fulton, his first owner. That attachment was why he'd insisted I purchase this house on his behalf.

And now I would be forcing him to leave it all behind.

I needed to do something special to commemorate our time here, to honor all this home had meant to us, all it had given us.

And I knew just the thing.

* * *

I'd hardly seen Charles these past few weeks as he prepared his firm for the transition in leadership. Fulton had helped us take care of that pesky detail as well. His daughter Bethany, a former colleague of ours, would be moving back to the Bay to transition from Longfellow & Associates to Peters & Associates.

I couldn't have selected a better person myself.

So while Charles worked feverishly to catch Bethany up on the current client load, I took care of things on the home front. Yes, I still wanted a career of my own, but I no longer wanted to force it. The right job would come to me at the right time, and until that happened, I had plenty to occupy my time with both the move and the baby.

We'd be selling the house furnished, which meant our packing would be minimal. It also meant that I had no trouble finding what I needed in the garden shed.

A hand shovel.

Carrying my prize, I walked around the perimeter of the house until I found the exact spot I needed. *Here.*

This was the scene of one of my earliest memories at the manor, so it made sense that it would also be one of my last.

I lowered myself onto my knees, leaned forward, and began to dig, creating a small pile of dirt beside me. It didn't take long to find what I was looking for, and I gasped with joy when the tip of my shovel hit the small coffin.

Well, really it was a shoe box.

Quickly clearing the rest of the dirt away with my fingers, I then lifted the dirty vessel from the ground, taking care not to disturb the lid.

I already knew what was inside, but I also understood that it wasn't my place to open it.

With great reverence, I brought the box inside. Charlene was already occupied with her lessons from the Sphynxes, which was just perfect for my purposes. I wanted to have this special moment alone with Octo-Cat.

I let myself into his bedroom, closing the door behind me so that we wouldn't be disturbed.

Octo-Cat turned from where he was watching his fish swim about the tank. "I'm going to miss these little guys."

"I know," was all I said. Logistically, we just couldn't move a one-hundred-and-forty gallon tank across the country. Luckily, our friend Frank at the pet supply store had agreed to give Yummy, Delicious, and the others a new home.

The tabby's eyes grew wide when he spotted what I held in my hands. "What's that?"

"It's a present. For you."

His nose turned up in disgust, drawing his whiskers together. "Angela, I can't accept that. It's filthy."

"You don't have to touch it, but I wanted you to have it." I removed the lid and placed the box on the floor so he could admire its contents. Inside lay several large pieces of floral-patterned Lenox. It was one of the late Ethel Fulton's teacups. Sure, Octo-Cat still had the others, but this one was special to him. It's why we had gone to the trouble of throwing a funeral when it got broken, and it's why I wanted him to have it now.

Back then I had rolled my eyes at the ridiculousness, but now I couldn't imagine leaving it behind. This broken teacup had become an important part of our family history, and it would be coming with us.

Octo-Cat sighed happily. "My long lost Evian vessel."

I smiled as I watched the realization take hold. "Yes."

"But why did you disturb its eternal slumber?"

"I thought you might want to bring it with us."

"It's true I miss Ethel very deeply, but you're my human now, Angela. And you're taking me to live beside my dearest Grizabella, which is the greatest thing a cat could ever want. I appreciate the gesture, but I don't need this anymore."

Honestly, his response wasn't what I'd expected, and I didn't want him to come to regret it later. "Are you sure?"

Octo-Cat shook his head. "We should let sleeping teacups lie. Why waste time digging up the past when the future is right there for us to grab with both paws?"

And honestly, I couldn't have said it better myself.

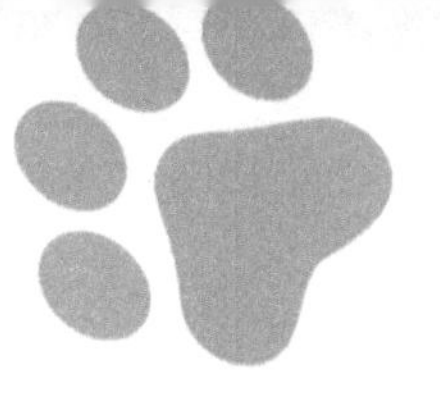

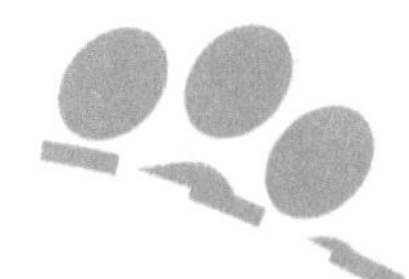

20

One week later, Charles and I flew out to Colorado, paying extra to bring the cats in cabin with us. Octo-Cat happily consented to medication to help bypass his nerves, which made the flight quite pleasant for the rest of us.

Charles had already worked with a dealership remotely to purchase a new car for each of us, having traded in our old models back in Maine. Which meant all we had to do now was to take a taxi straight from the airport to the dealership. I squealed with delight when the car salesman handed me the keys to my brand-new MINI Cooper. Charles had purchased a more sensible

SUV, but I wasn't ready for the mini-van life just yet.

For years, both Nan and Charles had pleaded with me to turn in my junky old jalopy for something new, and given the logistics of our move plus my fast-approaching motherhood, I'd finally listened. Making me wonder why I hadn't given in sooner.

I guess I had wanted to earn it myself rather than letting my grandmother, boyfriend, or cat pay the way. Charles finally convinced me to allow myself this small luxury by offering me a new car as celebration for my new job.

Yes, I'd gotten a job, and it was in the most round-about way possible. In preparation for our move, I reactivated my social media profile and started looking into local businesses I could support once we'd relocated. I even changed my town to Boulder, CO, and wouldn't you know it, I started to get served local ads for the area.

One of the ads featured my meme along with the words: *Animals talk. It's up to you to listen to what they have to say. Join us for a special talk with animal behaviorist Meredith Greyson. Admission is free, but donations to our shelter are highly encouraged.*

I decided to message the page that was sponsoring the event, an animal rescue group. I told them who I was and asked if I could get a recording of the event since I wouldn't yet be in town when Dr. Greyson gave her talk.

They recognized me from my profile picture, and it all escalated rather quickly from there and before I knew it, I was hired—not just hired, but they'd created a whole new position for me.

It would be up to me to help match the shelter pets with their perfect forever homes. I would use my talents to create robust adoption profiles detailing exactly what each animal wanted from his or her new family. I'd also be present at any meet-and-greets with potential pet parents to make sure it was a match on both sides.

The position was volunteer for now, but honestly I didn't need the money. I just wanted the purpose, and this one was absolutely perfect for me.

I started next week.

That gave Charles and me some time to settle into our new home. We had a lot of furniture shopping to do to fill up our new neo-colonial domicile. We'd bought in an up-and-coming community of other young families. Sure, our house was much smaller than what we'd had before, but we absolutely loved it.

The manor house had always felt like it belonged to Ethel. This new construction was all ours, and as a bonus it was situated in a great part of the city with loads of entertainment options, both for adults and kids. Just past the city, we had gorgeous scenery that reminded me of back home in Maine, though we were in a whole new mountain range now. We even had a small garden that reminded me of the inn in Virginia where we'd first met Charlene.

Best of all though, we would already have friends and family close by. Grandma Lyn had ordered a new build on the other side of our neighborhood and would be joining us when it was ready. Christine and Grizabella, on the other hand, were already here. Not only were they a short eight-minute drive away, but they were also *here* here, waiting for us now in the driveway of our new digs.

"Welcome home, you!" Christine screamed, racing forward to give me a hug.

"Let me out of here! I need to lick my wife!" Octo-Cat screamed from inside his carrier.

I returned my friend's hug briefly before racing

for the door. "Let's get the cats inside. They're eager to say hello."

Charles twisted the key in the lock and pushed the door open to reveal the spacious open-concept floor plan, and I loved the place even more now that I got to see it in person.

Yes, like our cars, we also bought our house sight unseen. Clearly, the builder's pictures hadn't done it justice. And now I twirled around, eager to take it all in.

"Angela!" Octo-Cat growled and shook his carrier, throwing himself against the metal door. "If you don't let me out this instant—"

I quickly stooped down to open the little door, and he flew forth like a madman.

"Um, Christine. You better let Grizabella out fast, or I'm not responsible for what Octavius does."

"Oh, yes, right." She held the Himalayan in a space-age looking backpack, which she easily maneuvered to one shoulder and unzipped.

Grizz hopped right out and ran to nuzzle her groom. "My darling! I can't believe you're really here!"

"Well, believe it, baby. I'm never leaving you again. I—"

"Octo-Papa?" Charlene's voice broke in, a soft and hesitant mewl.

Charles stood on the doorstep holding a small nylon carrier. I grabbed it from him and gently removed the little black kitten, setting her on the floor a few paces away from her adoptive parents.

"Oh, my sweet girl!" Grizabella cried and floated forward to slather her new daughter in sandpaper kisses. Both cats purred so loud, it was hard to hear anything else.

Until Octo-Cat came over and nudged me with his paw. I settled myself on the floor so that I could hear him, while Charles and Christine went outside to grab the Sphynxes.

"Would you look at the two of us?" he said, watching his two girls with obvious pride. "We did good, Angela. Real good."

I smiled as I scratched at the fur between his ears.

My heart felt full, but then he continued, "Honestly, I always knew I'd get my happy ending, but I didn't know whether you had it in you. I'm glad I was wrong."

I laughed and pushed myself to my hands and feet.

Charles and Christine had just released Jacques and Jillianne into the empty house, and the two hairless cats immediately ran upstairs to hide.

"Well, it may take them a little getting used to," I said, knowing I would do whatever they needed to help them accept this place as home.

I sauntered over to my husband and threw both arms around his shoulders, stealing a quick kiss. "Welcome home, Mr. Longfellow."

He kissed me again and said, "Welcome home, Mrs. Longfellow."

A light scratching at the door caused us to exchange a confused look.

"Were you expecting anyone else?" Christine asked, and we both shook our heads.

"Might as well see who it is," I announced as I padded toward the door and pulled it open.

A familiar masked bandit stood on my new porch step, stroking his tail and flashing a fanged smile my way. "You didn't seriously think you could go anywhere without me. Did you?" Pringle demanded, pushing his way into the house.

"But Pringle, how did you...?"

"I left early. The seagulls helped map my path, and from there, I just hitched rides in old truck beds. It's amazing how accommodating folks can be when they don't even know you're there."

"Well, I'm glad you're here," I told him. The trash panda had in fact disappeared days before our departure, and I'd worried that I'd never get the chance to see him again. Like Octo-Cat, I was glad I'd been wrong.

"We'd have brought you, but—"

"Yeah, yeah, it's illegal to own wildlife. Something about me being undomesticatable. Shows what they know!"

"I'd be happy to build you a treehouse out back," I offered. "But you know you can't stay in here."

"Just wanted to introduce myself as your new neighbor," he said, offering a wave and moving back toward the door. "Let me know when that treehouse is ready for me!" he called as I held the door open for him.

I shut the door again, and almost immediately my phone buzzed with an incoming call.

"Hi, Nan," I shouted happily.

"How was your flight? Did you make it? You forgot to call!"

"Oh, sorry. Yeah, we just got here, and, Nan, it's beautiful. You'll love it when you and Grant visit next month." Yes, we'd already planned out an entire year of visits, and, no, it probably wouldn't be enough.

"That's lovely, dear. I've been dying to tell you the news." Her voice dropped to a conspiratorial whisper that was hard to hear over the phone. "Grant and I drove by your old place, and the new people are already moving in."

"That's good. I hope they love it as much as we did."

"No, that's not the news." She paused for a beat, so dramatic my grandmothers. "Something's off about them. I'm sure of it."

"Off how?" I nibbled on my lower lip to keep from laughing.

Nan, however, remained undeterred. "I don't know. It's just a feeling I get. That something isn't right. Angie, I think we have a mystery on our hands."

I chuckled at that. "Oh, no you don't. I'm out of the mystery business now, remember? I'm now a pet placement specialist for the local animal shelter."

"You may be done with the mystery business, but I don't think I am," she revealed, making me wish this had been a FaceTime call instead of voice only.

"What are you trying to say?" I asked slowly.

"How upset would you be if I revived Pet Whisperer, P.I.?"

"Not upset, but Nan, that's a thing of the past. Besides," I reminded her, "you can't talk to animals."

"It's all about branding. You never wanted people to know you could either, dear. And besides, whether or not you like it, you've built up all this notoriety now. We can't just let that go. I know, how about Pet Whisperer, Incorporated? It's different but the same as all great business ideas are."

When I realized she was one-hundred-percent serious, I finally relented. "I think that has a nice ring to it. If you want it, it's all yours."

"Angie dear, I don't think I have a choice," came her immediate reply.

And that's how my business died and then came back to life under new ownership. I'd gotten all I needed from my years as the Pet Whisperer. I couldn't wait to see what my kooky nan did with the title.

You haven't seen the last of Angie, Octo-Cat, and the gang. Nan is getting her own spin-off

series, Pet Whisperer INC. Can she fill Angie's shoes as Blueberry Bay's new resident sleuth?

* * *

Pssst… If you absolutely loved this book and want even more, check out Molly's Cozy Kitty Club for behind-the-scenes trivia and bonus scenes you won't find anywhere else!

WHAT TO READ NEXT!

My name is Gracie Springs, and I am not a witch…
but I'm pretty sure my cat is. I first started to get
suspicious when he jumped just a little too high
while chasing after a robin in our front yard. I knew
for sure when he opened up his mouth and
addressed me by name!

The first thing he told me? That he doesn't like the
name I gave him—even though "Fluffy" fits him
like a warm sweater at Christmas. Now we've
compromised on "Merlin the Magical Fluff," which
according to him references his long and proud
lineage just fine.

After that small matter was settled, he informed me that I must uphold his secret or risk spending the rest of my life in some magical prison. I agreed, not knowing it would turn into a full-time job of covering his tracks and fibbing our way out of some pretty tight spots.

When my boss at the local coffee shop turns up dead as a dormouse, things go from challenging to practically impossible... especially since all my coworkers seem to think I'm to blame.

Here's hoping my witchy cat can charm our way out of this one, because right now it looks like I'm cursed if I do and charged with murder if I don't. Yikes!

MERLIN TAKES A FAMILIAR is now available.

Get your copy so that you can start reading this zany mystery series today!

My name is Gracie Springs, and I've always been a pretty normal girl. I work as a barista while working toward my master's degree in Sociology. I've finished all my coursework but still haven't landed upon the perfect thesis topic. And I can't earn my degree until I do.

Oops.

Meanwhile I live in a small suburban town in Southern Georgia called Elderberry Heights. And the name fits it to a *T,* because most of my neighbors are somewhere north of seventy years old. I'm living in my grandma Grace's house, which she left behind when she chose to move south to a trendy retirement community in the Florida Keys.

She gave me the home where she raised my

father and all my uncles, saying it was my early inheritance and that I'd always been her favorite, anyway—and not just because we shared a name.

She left all her furniture and decor, which means my house has at least three dozen hand-crocheted doilies and the living room is made up of brown floral couches and honey oak side tables. I don't have the heart—or the money—to change anything.

Grandma Grace also left me this ragamuffin cat that turned up at her doorstep only days before she'd been scheduled to move out and me to move in. The vet says he's a Maine Coon. I say he's much larger than any cat should ever be, especially considering all that stripey fur that poofs out from his body and makes him look like a literal fluff ball.

I guess that's why I named him Fluffy.

Keeping a cat I hadn't wanted was a small price to pay for being handed a free house, and over time Fluffy has started to grow on me. He's not exactly the cuddly type. In fact, every time, I've tried to pick him up, he's gone for blood. And succeeded in getting it twice.

I don't try to pick him up anymore, but if I sit really still and pretend I'm not interested, sometimes he'll help himself to my lap. Once he even purred.

Fluffy does love food and often takes a bite of whatever I'm having for dinner. He also enjoys running up and down the hallways in the middle of the night like a creature possessed.

I hadn't meant for him to be an outdoor cat, but he's such a good escape artist that eventually I just installed a pet door so I wouldn't have to worry about it, anymore.

That brings me to this morning...

I was running late for work, thanks to having a particularly difficult time following a new makeup tutorial from my favorite beauty Tuber. In the end, I scrubbed off the whole thing and went with a smoky eye and nude lip. That'd teach me to try something new so close to the start of my shift.

Especially since my mean old boss would take any excuse to dock my pay. He's still bitter that a popular franchised cafe moved in a couple streets away and cut his profits considerably. But he's also stubborn and not quite ready to admit defeat, which is why he's kept the whole staff on while slashing our hours and looking for any excuse to pay us less.

Great guy, that boss of mine.

I hadn't seen Fluffy since breakfast and wanted

to make sure everything was okay with him before taking off for my shift.

"Fluffy! Fluffy! Here, kitty, kitty!" I called and clicked my tongue, but he didn't come running. He never comes running. It's always up to me to find him.

And so I looked under the bed, behind the couch, and out the front window.

Finally I spotted him with his butt in the air and face toward the ground in that classic pre-pounce pose. Across the way stood an unaware robin bathing in the stone birdbath Grandma left behind with whatever few drops hadn't yet been evaporated by the hot summer sun.

Wiggle, wiggle, went Fluffy's butt.

He leaped, but the robin saw him coming and flittered away.

Fluffy flittered after him.

Not just a normal cat leap, either. He looked like a tiny feline athlete about to slam dunk a basketball. Up and up he went after that frightened avian target. He must have gone at least six feet into the sky and was still climbing up, up, up.

That's when he turned his head my way and saw me watching. Those emerald eyes bored straight into mine, and for a moment he remained stuck mid-jump just hanging in the air.

Then he turned again, and the sudden movement broke the spell. Fluffy came crashing straight back to earth, then skittered out of sight, leaving me to wonder: *What in the heck just happened?*

* * *

I chalked the whole gravity-defying cat episode up to poor sleep and an overactive imagination, then hurried my way over to Harold's House of Coffee.

Despite ignoring both speed limits and stop signs, I wound up three minutes late for my shift. My boss, Harold himself, stood just inside the front door waiting for me.

He tapped his wrist even though he never wore a watch and shouted, "When will you learn? Three minutes means three dollars, and since this is your second offense this week, I'm doubling it."

I snorted and rushed past him to clock in.

"Gracie! Aren't you listening to me?" he demanded, trailing after me like a demented duckling.

"Yes, you're docking me six dollars for being three minutes late, even though we have no customers and you only pay us minimum wage. And even that's because you're legally obligated. Pretty soon I'm going to be paying you for the pleasure of standing around with nothing to do while our customers hang out at Mermaid's Brew down the street. Does that sound about right?"

Harold's face turned bright red. "The insolence!" he screamed. "If it didn't cost so much to train someone new, you'd be out of a job. In fact you're lucky that I—"

He took a step back, shook his head, and tried again. "Listen here, Gracie. You're lucky that—"

His words stopped coming as he gasped and crumpled to the floor. From hotheaded to out cold in mere seconds.

"Harold, Harold!" I cried and fell to my knees to check if he was breathing.

He wasn't.

I grabbed his wrist and tried to find a pulse.

I couldn't.

Ruh-oh.

MERLIN TAKES A FAMILIAR is now available.

Get your copy so that you can start reading this zany mystery series today!

ABOUT MOLLY FITZ

While *USA Today bestselling* author Molly Fitz can't technically talk to animals, she and her three feline writing assistants have deep and very animated conversations as they navigate their days.

She lives with her child and their own private zoo somewhere in the wilds of Alaska. Molly will occasionally venture out for good food, great coffee, or to meet new animal friends.

Learn more about Molly and her books, and be sure to sign up for her newsletter at **www.Molly Mysteries.com**.

ALSO BY MOLLY FITZ

Learn more about Molly's collected works, so that you can decide which book you'd like to read next...

PET WHISPERER P.I.

Angie Russo just partnered up with Blueberry Bay's first ever talking cat detective. Along with his ragtag gang of human and animal helpers, Octo-Cat is determined to save the day... so long as it doesn't interfere with his schedule.

Start with book 1, ***Kitty Confidential***.

MERLIN'S MAGICAL MYSTERIES

Gracie Springs is not a witch... but her cat is. Now she must help to keep his secret or risk spending the rest of her life in some magical prison. Too bad trouble seems to find them at every turn!

Start with book 1, ***Merlin Takes a Familiar***.

PARANORMAL TEMP AGENCY

Tawny Bigford's simple life takes a turn for the magical when she stumbles upon her landlady's murder and is recruited by a talking black cat named Fluffikins to take over the deceased's role as the official Town Witch for Beech Grove, Georgia.

Start with book 1, ***Witch for Hire***.

THE MYSTERIES OF MOONLIGHT MANOR (WITH TRIXIE SILVERTALE)

Sydney Coleman has it all—until she doesn't. No sooner does she launch her bed and breakfast, than a trio of ghosts turn up oppose her at every turn. They insist she solve the murder of their mistress, but Sydney is desperate for cash. If she can't book some guests fast, her haunted mansion is utterly doomed.

Start with book 1, ***Moonlight & Mischief***.

CONNECT WITH MOLLY

Sign up for my newsletter and get a special digital prize pack for joining, including an exclusive story, *Meowy Christmas Mayhem*, fun quiz, and lots of cat pictures!

Sign up: **MollyMysteries.com/subscribe**

Now, if you ever wished you could converse with cats, here's your opportunity! This is me officially inviting you into my whacky inner world as part of my Cozy Kitty Book Club.

For those who just can't get enough of my zany cat characters and their hapless humans, this book club will provide new content to devour and the chance to get to know my best author friends.

From exclusive stories, behind-the-scenes trivia to never-before-released bonus content, and monthly giveaways, there's a lot to love about the Cozy Kitty Book Club. Join today to find out what we're reading next!

Join: **MollyMysteries.com/club**

www.ingramcontent.com/pod-product-compliance
Lightning Source LLC
Chambersburg PA
CBHW022032120726

47899CB00007BA/2349